American Dream

1st Edition 1st December 2017

Authors Note

This tale is divided into three Parts or Phases of my life characterised by the Yiddish. Schlepper, Macher, and Mensch.

Part 1. Schlepper: My apprenticeship, growing up and learning from my parents, teachers, and surroundings.

Part 2. Macher: Becoming a husband, a father, a leader and innovator in construction.

Part 3. Mensch. Becoming a philosopher with a global perspective, looking back, making sense of what has happened, and finding a way based on what I have learned. Allowing for the fact, I am less physically able than in my Macher phase.

This is the story of a family from the dark days of life after the Second World War to the present day. The family have left the poor living they had as farmers in Scotland to look for a better life in California, USA. The story has many twists and turns from the West coast to the East coast. It reflects the difficulties families' face, the battle to survive in an economy with peaks and troughs. The need to find a place called "home".

This is the story of a life. It is written as a screenplay because I happen to be reading a screenplay. (Perfect Days by Liz Lochhead) Other influences that I am reading are the Rises & falls of the Royal Stewarts by Oliver Thomson, Murakhami, Paul Theroux,

PART 1 SCHLEPPER

Chapter 1	**Malibu**	**Page 5**
Chapter 2	**Mum and Dad**	**Page 10**
Chapter 3	**Chicago**	**Page 13**
Chapter 4	**School Days**	**Page 16**
Chapter 5	**Holidays**	**Page 18**
Chapter 6	**Mum and Dad**	**Page 20**
Chapter 7	**Chicago, Early 1970s**	**Page 26**
Chapter 8	**San Francisco, Late 1970s**	**Page 29**
Chapter 9	**Anthrax**	**Page 33**
Chapter 10	**San Francisco carpenter**	**Page 36**
Chapter 11	**South Africa**	**Page 39**
Chapter 12	**College San Francisco**	**Page 44**
Chapter 13	**Vermont**	**Page 46**
Chapter 14	**Manhattan**	**Page 50**

PART 2 MACHER

Chapter 15	**Daisy**	**Page 53**
Chapter 16	**Leyla**	**Page 55**
Chapter 17	**Black Monday**	**Page 59**
Chapter 18	**Bekka, Rockport**	**Page 62**
Chapter 19	**Jim, Rockport**	**Page 64**

Chapter 20	**Divorce**	**Page 67**
Chapter 21	**San Francisco, again**	**Page 70**
Chapter 22	**Millennium, Sophia**	**Page 74**
Chapter 23	**Mystic, Lily**	**Page 77**
Chapter 24	**Lily**	**Page 85**
Chapter 25	**San Francisco with Lily**	**Page 89**

PART 3 MENSCH

Chapter 26	**Scotland**	**Page 95**
Chapter 27	**San Francisco, Full Circle**	**Page 98**
Chapter 28	**Western Isles**	**Page 98**
Chapter 29	**Penninghame Journal**	**Page 106**
	Levellers Diet	**Page 118**
	Silly Wee Poems	**Page 132**
	Tracks of my Years	**Page 142**
	Last Will and Testament	**Page 144**

PART 1 SCHLEPPER

Chapter 1 Malibu

The story starts in the 1950s in Malibu, California and continues to the present day.

CAST

AJ McClain	Myself
Noel McClain	Dad, Veterinarian and former Pilot
Mary Maxwell	Mum, Dental receptionist
Deirdre Portus	Granny, Artist, beekeeper, gardener
William Portus	Uncle Willy, Fisherman, story teller, Canada
May McClain	Aunty May, Social worker

The scene is Tierra Nova, Malibu, a large beach house on the cliffs overlooking the North Pacific Ocean and the Saratoga hills.

The USA was a very different place in the 1950s. The 2nd World War 1939 -1945 was 10 years ago and life was developing slowly from the horrors and deprivation of war. It was the summer of 1956. Mum & Dad got married the previous year in Malibu. Grandfather died in the early summer 27/06/56 at the age of 89. We never met as I was born in September 1956. He was a huge figure in Malibu, soldier, attorney, writer, mayor, and mountaineer; a big influence on me. He and Granny had migrated from Scotland at the turn of the century where they had earned a poor living farming. They were pioneers in the new world that was California. Grandfather eventually became a successful attorney to the early film industry in Hollywood.

August 1956 Deirdre (67) is a rather eccentric artist, mother of May, Douglas, Noel & Paul. She has had to get used to a lot of changes recently with the death of her husband in June. The children have grown up. May a spinster still lives with her at Tierra Nova. Noel has returned with his new wife Mary now heavily pregnant. Noel is a young veterinarian, following his service towards the end of World War 2 as a Catalina pilot based at Pensacola, Florida.

Willie (68) is Deirdre's older brother. Bit of a mystery man. He had a life & family in Canada but is now living back at Tierra Nova. He has a routine lunching at the diner (Deirdre sometimes serves up meals that are not to his liking), golfing, and fishing.

It's a sunny morning in August. Willie and Deirdre are out the back of the house (which is actually the front.) Deirdre is pottering about her beloved sweet peas accompanied by Kimmy the dog. Willie is sat on a bench in the sun tending to his fishing tackle.

Willie: Don't think I will go fishing today Deirdre. The ocean surf is not good for fishing. *He has 3 tins of tackle on the bench he is tending to.* When the wind is light and the tide full in. That will be my time.

Deirdre: You be careful in the ocean. You know how quickly it can change and you are not as steady on your feet as you were. Kimmy leave my sweet peas you bad dog. I will need to go in soon to make lunch. It's like having a family again with you May, Mary & Noel.

Noel: Well it's a fine day. How's the fishing tackle Willie?

Willie: I'm not as good as I was. Can't see so well and I'm not so nimble. *The tins are bright coloured bait, some tiny, some large. Beautiful colors made of feather and hair.*

Noel: Mary is putting her feet up at the front. She's feeling quite uncomfortable now. I cannot wait for this baby to come.

Willie: I wonder if it will be a boy or a girl and have you thought of any names?

Deirdre: There are old ways of telling if it's a boy or a girl. I don't think you need to worry about a girl's name. Come on Kimmy lets go and make some lunch. Are you hungry Noel?

Noel looks at Willie with a pained look.

Willie: Nothing for me Deirdre I will eat at the diner.

Deirdre: Anyone would think you don't like my cooking.

Willie: Not at all Deirdre I just need to stretch my legs.

Deirdre: Noel, is salad ok for you? Can you tell Mary & May we are having lunch.

Mary & May are on sun loungers at the front of the house.

May: How are we feeling today Mary? (In a matronly way)

Mary: We are feeling very hot and uncomfortable as you can see.

May: Can I get you anything, a glass of water perhaps?

Mary: No that's ok thanks May. I will just sit quietly reading and waiting for baby to arrive.

May: Well it's a lovely day and doesn't the ocean look fine. All that spoils it is the bees. I wish mum would not keep the hives so close to the house.

Mary: They won't harm you if you leave them be.

Noel: Well you two. Are you ready for lunch?

Mary: Yes I am hungry. I am eating for two.

Noel: Deirdre's started preparing lunch.

Mary: Oh May can you give her a hand. She raises her eyebrows. She knows that Deirdre is no chef.

May: Mother is an artist. She can be a bit eccentric in her way of working.

Noel: Now you two. Its salad I think. What can go wrong?

Mary: Again! Noel, can we go out for dinner this evening?

Noel helps Mary get up and they go to sit down in the dining area for lunch.

Deirdre has prepared lunch of vegetable broth, bread. A salad of lettuce, celery, tomatoes from the garden, spam, hard boiled eggs, all basic wholesome stuff, and fruit to follow. Quite nice but often repeated.

Deirdre: There we are then. May can you say grace.

May: Bless us, oh Lord and these thy gifts which we are about to receive from thy bounty through Christ our Lord. Amen

Mary looks at Noel ruefully.

Noel: Tuck in Mary. Have you got your bag packed for hospital? You are close to your due date.

Mary: Just as well you are a vet in case the baby comes before we get there. Doctor says I should go into hospital early because my blood pressure is high and it's such a long way.

May: I thought you might have the baby here?

Mary: I thought about it. I'll be better served in hospital with my blood pressure and all.

(Whispers to Noel) Change of diet might help.

Deirdre: Come on Mary. Have some more. Plain food is good for you and the baby.

May: Yes Mary you really must.

Mary: Just an apple please.

Noel: Willie has asked me to join him for 9 holes this afternoon.

Mary: Alright for some fly boy.

Noel: I don't have to.

Deirdre: It will do you good Noel. You work hard helping all the dear animals.

Chapter 2 Mum and Dad

Noel went to school in LA which he liked and to boarding school in Seattle which he spoke of little so I assume he was not so fond of this. This was the way of things for the children of an eminent attorney in these days. They wanted the children to be well educated so they could aspire to a professional career. Noel was born in June 1924 so by 1941 the 2nd World War was in full force and Noel was 17. He like many of his age volunteered for service. He volunteered to join the US air force to train as a pilot. He had the necessary skill and aptitude and quickly won his wings and progressed from small planes to crew on bombers. In 1944 the USA came into the war. Neill got the opportunity to pilot Catalina sea planes for the US Navy. He trained at Pensacola in Florida and on the great lakes. The war ended before he saw service. This could well have saved his life. Like many of his generation, on completion of service, they preferred not to speak about it. They had to grow up quick. They wanted to move on. To forget the bad things that happened. Prisoners of war had suffered and died in great numbers. When the war came to an end in 1945 Noel was thankfully unscathed apart from a thumb he could bend right back. A Canadian accidently shot him during training on the rifle ranges. He then had to think about what to do. The plan was probably for Noel to go into the family firm as an attorney. But after the experience of war and his love of animals he decided otherwise. He did not wish to concern himself with the frailties of man. He wanted to be a veterinarian. He was 23 by now and on his return to Malibu he had to go back to school to finish his education. He was living at the family home Walnut House which he was very fond of. It would take Noel another 5 years to complete his education and qualify as a veterinarian.

During his time on secondment at a veterinary practice in Boston he met Mary. She was working as a dental receptionist for a local dentist. Mary was tall, dark, good looking, an accomplished swimmer having worked previously at a local outdoor pool. She was a great story teller and a bit of a rebel. She said she knew Sean Connery and was a political activist. Mary had no family to speak of (and it wasn't) and remains a mystery to this day. Noel spent more time than he had to at the dentist and he and Mary started courting and were married in Malibu in 1955. Noel was 31 and Mary was 24.

It's a bit unclear who Noel was working for in 1956 when they were living at Tierra Nova but knowing my mother she would not be there for long. She would want her own home!

fineart
america

Chapter 3 Chicago

E 73rd Chicago, 30 September 1959. It's my 3rd Birthday and I can almost form my own memories. I was born in LA and lived at Tierra Nova, Malibu for a short while. Dad got a job as a vet at a practice in Canada. My brother John was born there on 20 May 1958 (the only Canadian in the family). My mother loved it there. But she always said that. They had a black standard poodle called Juno. We lived in a town house in E 73rd. You went up steps off the busy road. In those days it wasn't all cars. I can remember tradesmen coming to the door to sell their wares and looking for scrap. Onion Johnnies with great strings of onions suspended from all points of their bike. Brush salesmen, knife sharpeners. Much of Old Chicago was being demolished and re developed around what would become a large university campus. Printing, publishing and the new world port was the mainstay of the city at the time. 1959 was a big year. Queen Elizabeth 11 came to town. There was a big parade. Being of Scottish heritage we were there waving our flags. It was a hot summer and a cold winter with snow. It was very different to Malibu The house was 3 storeys. Initially the veterinary surgery was in the basement. The practice was called Blackhill & McClain. I always got the impression that Blackhill did a lot better from it than McClain. There was a small garden at the back that looked over the city to the Chicago River. Most of my memories of that time are of playing in the sand pit in the back garden with my brother John. Up and down stairs, linoleum floors. It was simply furnished with none of the modern conveniences we have now. No TV until 1959. There was no colour TV and not much colour in our surroundings. It was cold in the winter. There was no central heating. The windows were freezing and wet. There was no double glazing. But we were happy. I think. I remember mum having a few vinyl records. Bill Hailey and his Comets; Francoise Hardy. Douglas was born in that house on 13 April 1960. We had arrived in the swinging 60's. I can remember John, I and others clambering in the hall outside the room where Douglas was born waiting for news.

Nursery School: Looking back Mum & Dad were middle class, influenced by the Royal Family. Our Scottish heritage never left us. You can see it in early family photos. I went to nursery school when I was three years old. Some of the infants in my class were still in my class at High School 14 years later.

Cedar Road, Chicago. Things were moving fast. The 50s was a period of hardship and finding our feet after the war. The 60s was a time of growth and rapid change. It certainly was for us. We had outgrown our home on E 73rd. We moved up river to a nice home in the suburbs. The practice moved to new premises in the city. Business was good. Dad looked after the welfare of farm animals and pets. Dad & his partner bought new cars. They bought identical Chevrolet estates, one with a red stripe on the side, one with a white stripe on the side. This was for identification purposes. Farmers would flag them down if they had an emergency. Oak Park was more similar in size to Malibu and we thrived there. Our house was a traditional detached on the corner of Trail Street with a nice big garden. The 60s was a time of great changes for Chicago. Industry was thriving. Areas that were undeveloped or swamp were developed. A short walk from our home was many areas of land under development. No tarmac roads or services and homes being built by the local builder. At the time there were no boundary fences or security. These areas were an adventure playground for children. Parents at the time were not worried about their children going out. It was common for a child to have older brothers or sisters to keep an eye on them. Neighbouring families would get to know each other and children would form gangs (in a nice way). The building sites became ours in the evenings and at weekends. There were great mounds of sand, gravel, and earth to make dens and defend. There were homes in construction to explore. Scaffold to climb. There was an abundant supply of brick's and timber for building dens. The occasional threat of a neighbour or builder telling us we should not be there. Or a gang we did not know so well coming on our patch. There are a couple of incidents at this time that remain. When it rained heavily, rivers were formed down the unmade roads on the site. It was our pleasure to form dams in the river and small lakes. By this time a few homes were now occupied by new residents. One in particular was not to our liking. He came out his newly painted front door and shouted at us to clear off. I am not proud of this. I made a ball of mud slurry from our dam. I threw it at his closing door with all my strength. It made a terrible mess. Realising the gravity of what

I had done. I signalled for all to grab bikes if they had them and run. On another occasion we were forming an expedition to a more distant site on the way to Claypots neighbourhood. This was more challenging as we would come across unknown and possibly more threatening gangs, and unfamiliar hazards. We were in a group outside the Main twins house (I recall there seemed to be a lot of twins around in those days) and my brother John wanted to go home. At this stage I was his guardian being two years older. I did a quick risk assessment and figured he could find his own way home. I sent him on his way. Later I went home. Nobody was at home. Mum was shopping. Dad was at work. I went next door to the Pagets. He was not there. Well the balloon went up. The Pagets were a large family who lived next door. They had two sets of twins eventually. Mr Paget was a tall, stern teacher at the Academy.

Me: Hello Mrs Paget there's nobody in at home. Is John here?

Mrs Paget: No I haven't seen him. Where was he last?

As my story unravelled Mrs Paget was looking more alarmed and angry. We were in the kitchen.

Mrs Paget: Sit in that chair and don't move.

Now I can't remember whether they had a phone. Not everybody did. But neighbours were contacted, my parent's, the cops.

Mrs Paget: You are a bad, bad boy and you know what bad boys get.

In her case I did. She produced the wooden spoon from the table drawer and gave me a sharp rap on each hand. John thankfully was eventually returned by the cops. He had walked all the way down to the shore before being found by the cops and returned. I guess he was three or 4 years old at the time. The interim period spent confined to Mrs Paget's kitchen is not a pleasant memory. More unpleasantness from my parents followed. My relationship with my brother changed after that. I realised that being the eldest had a downside. My brother could be a liability that could do me harm. I do not think we had so much freedom after that. Also the area was becoming more developed and not such a playground.

Chapter 4 School Days

School days, Chicago. I briefly went to the Academy in 1960. On my 1st day of school in August I was not yet five years old my birthday being 30 September. Mum had made all the preparations for my 1st day. Uniform, up early, both nicely turned out for the half mile walk to school. Mrs Paget was taking care of John & Doug. Now I don't know why but events took an important turn that would affect the rest of our lives. And I'm not proud of this. It's probably had a profound effect to this day. When we were within site of the school gate I decided I wasn't going. To the extent that I sat on the pavement, crying and generally being awful. I seem to remember being in the classroom but you could say I didn't settle in. I have probably blotted the worst excesses from my memory but I wasn't there for long. What happened next was fate which had far reaching consequences. I guess it was difficult for Mum and Dad to know what to do next. Well I ended up going to Chicago High where term started a month later. This was a massive change. Chicago High is a fee paying school in the city. It was half an hour's drive from where we lived. The Academy was the local state school. I suppose I feel ashamed about that. I was the eldest and should have set a better example. Going to this school also made me much more aware of class & politics. Chicago was a working class city and the 60s was the era of injustice to workers, peace and love, race & teenage rebellion, and the Beatles. I increasingly became ashamed of being middle class and going to a fee paying school and inclined towards rebellion. Unfortunately I would never know how I would have fared at the Academy. So now I was in Primary 1 at Chicago High. Miss Day was my teacher. I can't remember whether I settled in there more easily. Perhaps the fact that I knew some children from nursery helped. I had to change my uniform. It was a very traditional education. We learned our times tables; a-z; coloured rods. We were taught slowly & methodically. I remember occasions when I required individual attention. I was left handed. I had my own way of going up and down stairs that required some changing. I went to elocution lessons. I wanted to be good. I tried. I would often be disappointed that I was not as good as expected. I assume there was much discussion between my parents about what they were now taking on. There were school fees to pay for three children and one more to come. Dad now had the additional responsibility of driving me to school and would do this for the next 18 years in addition to his job. John & Doug went to Chicago High by default. So every other year the poor teachers had a McClain in their class. I don't think there was anything in it but the fact you had brothers there was not publicised. Occasionally I had to take on elder responsibilities. It was normal for brothers & sisters to walk past each other in the corridor or playground with scarcely a glance.

Chapter 5 Holidays

Holidays, California. Whenever there was a school holiday we would pile into whatever car we had at the time ranging from the Chevy, Ford, Dodge and more. There were mixed blessings on going on holiday. The boot of Dads car was always full of what we called "drugs" all the equipment a vet needs on farms and for small animals. This cocktail of equipment had a smell of its own which remained with you. It was a long drive to Malibu with motel stops. Somebody or other was inevitably car sick. We often stayed at the trailer park. No ordinary trailer park. It was a beautiful estate with private beaches. The trailers were placed discreetly among the pines overlooking the beach. This would become our new adventure playground. Our freedom to roam at home was diminishing. We could swim in the sea, go sailing, and build sandcastles on the beach. We could surf, go fishing. There was a little island to explore. We were allowed to roam there. We had many adventures on the beach. It was like the adventures of Huckleberry Finn.

In the early days (which it seemed were in black & white) we would spend more time at Tierra Nova visiting Granny & Uncle Willie & Auntie May. For a small child this could be boring but there was plenty to observe. They would tell us stories of the old days in Scotland before the family emigrated. We children found them strange and other worldly. They were quite eccentric to us. Kimmy the dog, was old and eccentric too. It was interesting because it was so different to what I was used to. I liked to explore the rambling garden that looked down on the ocean. The sweet peas and bee hives were interesting. I always remember Uncle Willie sitting on a bench at the back door. Kind eyed old man with skin like brown shoe leather. He was always dressed in country clothes suitable for a colder climate. He was always doing some maintenance on his golf clubs or fishing tackle ready for the next outing. He would sometimes be oiling his old push along lawn mower before cutting the grass. I can still remember the smell of the oil mingled with the new cut grass in the sun. If I was lucky he would take me along fishing in the ocean. At that time there was plenty fish to be caught in the ocean. We would surf cast from the beach or the rocks. We loved casting into the foaming ocean, running back to avoid the swell, shouting to each other above the noise of the breaking waves. I would run up and down the beach, whooping and jumping with excitement, when Willie caught a fish. Golfing was with a half set of hickory shafted clubs. 9 holes were enough. There was a little path through a gate at the end of the garden through the woods. To the left it went down to the diner. Willies retreat at lunch time. To the right the path with a curious rope handrail wound its way down to the beach over a suspension footbridge built in 1911. As you went in the kitchen door at Tierra Nova there were steps and a small larder which was interesting. It was stocked with home-made jams and chutneys Deirdre and May made. The house itself had a lot of pine wood panelling and floors in evidence, and cottage windows. The walls were covered in lovely paintings of local landscapes, flowers, and fruit painted by Deirdre. It was designed to remind them of Scotland in some ways. As you moved through the house, wood floors and stairs creaked, and clocks which were everywhere ticked, on the hour a cuckoo popped out from the clock from Switzerland. This was all different to what I was used to and very interesting. I was familiar with Heidi, the story of the little girl that lived in a chalet up a mountain in Switzerland, and that's what it felt like to me. We would sometimes sleep there, upstairs in metal springy old beds with eiderdowns. There was many family & friends to visit in Malibu. We liked to run to the playpark and visit Mr and Mrs Mathieson who always spoiled us. We would join the Mathieson's and their friends on the beach at Paradise Cove. I was known as Brambles then. Aunt May by then had a pink trailer at the beach. Dad's brother Paul and family would often be there on holiday at the same time as we were. Dad's older brother Douglas tragically died aged fifteen, after a football injury became infected. Antibiotics were rare at the time. His leg was amputated to try to stop the spread of infection. Sadly he died.

Chapter 6 Mum and Dad

Camphill Road, Chicago. I am guessing we moved here after Jean was born. (12 August 1964) The family had outgrown Cedar Road. Our little sister arrived four years after Doug. Mum had an unfortunate miscarriage in between times. Dad's solution to make mum feel better was to buy two cocker spaniel puppies Susy & Sally. It helped and they became a part of the family. The house was more like a mansion to us although it was split into three we had the biggest portion. Our home had a basement and a rambling garden on a hill overlooking the Chicago River. A pattern was developing of us moving on average every five years. This was not a good thing as we will see later. The basement was our play area. The previous occupants had left a pianola there. That is a piano that played itself. We had never seen one. The garden was steep and Dad would spend a lot of time forming terraces and a pond. This would be significant later. My brother became a landscape gardener.

Dalhousie Road, Chicago 1970. The family prospered during the 60's but started to struggle during the 70's. Private schooling costs were increasing (4 children at Chicago High). Large families were not so common now due to the cost. We had got used to middle class ways in the 60's. Dads business was changing. Farm work was less than it had been. Ministry of Agriculture work decreased. Farmers reduced costs by calling for veterinarians services as a last resort. He now worked with pets more than farm animals. Industrial Chicago was disappearing. Ship yards and traditional industries were closing. The oil industry had largely bypassed Chicago. Unemployment was rising. The move to Dalhousie Rd was a move down rather than a move up. It was a smaller house needing a lot of work done. Despite the economic outlook, Dad ploughed on trying to provide the family with everything. About this time another expensive item entered our lives. We all went to the local stables to have horse riding lessons. This became a passion for the family. I was not so passionate. I prefer horse power and horse racing. I have never learnt to trust anything with a pulse. Dads answer to mums desire to maintain middle class standards was to work harder. Mum and my brothers and sister started to spend their spare time at the stables. They progressed to buying clothing and tack. They bought a horse. They bought another one. They needed transport for the horses. They needed their own place for the horses. Dad was pleased because it kept the family happy. He took an interest in the horses. The horse fraternity came to him for treatment more than they had.

Long Grove, Illinois 1975. Horse riding by now was a big part of family life. Lonsdale was a small holding with a bungalow, stables, sheds, and fields. By now we had horses of our own, horse transport, and everything that goes with it. Where was the money coming from? I have no idea but I don't think it was sustainable. I was still routed in Chicago. I observed the horse business from a distance. I never got the bug.

Moncur, Illinois 1980. By now my siblings have left school. Dad no longer has the burden of school fees. He no longer has horses to pay for. I suspect by now he is relying on selling homes and paying off debt at the bank to keep his head above water. He has never shared financial matters with Mum. In those days it was normal for the man of the house to take care of work and bills. The woman looked after the children and the household. Things were changing and more women were going to work and having smaller families. Mum suffered from depression. Dad did not understand. He tried to make things better for her but it didn't seem to work. He liked to go to work. He spent long hours at work. Mum liked making a home and the children. That wasn't enough. She still had regular bouts of depression. The horses gave her a focus for a while but it wasn't enough. I worried about what would happen when Dad retired. Things were bad enough with no children at home and no horses. The latest plan was to sell Lonsdale. Sell the business. Rent a nearby farmhouse Moncur and build a retirement home in Long Grove. Pay some money to the bank. During this time Jean met Philip Richardson and got married. Philip was from a much richer family than us. The wedding was to be a lavish affair. It was traditional for the bride's father to pay for this. This tradition is, not so much the case recently. Dad confided in me the morning of the wedding. He had used a large chunk of the money he had set aside for his retirement home, for the wedding. I had just arrived back for the wedding from San Francisco. This shocking news changed my mood. I could not enjoy the wedding. I was surrounded by people I didn't know. They were all tucking into a splendid feast. I got drunk quickly and was helped to my room early by my brother. Dad managed the building of the new home, with an architect friend. I tried to offer some advice but I don't think he listened. When the house was finished it was very nice. It took longer to build than planned. It looked an expensive house. By the time he moved in he had not achieved his plan to repay the bank.

Long Grove, Illinois 1989. Dad is at an age when he should be retiring. He has served his country during war time. He has worked hard all his adult life. He has not accumulated any wealth. He owes the bank. Is this the American Dream? Mum continues to live a comfortable life. By now it is plain for her to see money is hard to come by. Her health issues continue. They continue moving house regularly. Mum seems to demand a move more often now. After about 3 years living in their retirement home Mum and Dad decide to move again.

California 1995 Not sure what prompted this move but there was talk of mum opening a coffee shop. However Dad was still under a lot of pressure from the bank despite being beyond retirement age. The house they bought was a rambling wreck of a place with a huge garden. I believe Dad continued working in Chicago and stayed at Doug's. Mum was Project Manager on the house but it was way too much to cope with. Emotionally she was not up to it. The house was not fit to live in and so she had to move to the Motel across the road. Eventually it was completed to a lovely standard as usual. I did not ask how things were at the bank. With Dad this was always a closely guarded secret. So ultimately the coffee shop never happened. Dad opened a surgery in the house and carried on working. I think he was still being granted mortgages beyond retirement age.

California 2000. I do not know the details of this move but suspect things were still not working out for Mum & Dad. Mum was not happy and Dad was still under pressure from bank. They moved to Paradise Cove. This was basically a move to pay back the bank. By now all the previous generation had passed and Tierra Nova sold sadly.

Chesterton, Indiana 2005. This was a last throw of the dice for Mum & Dad. The last property they had was sold to satisfy the bank. Mum had finally realised she had no family nearby in Malibu. She wanted to be closer to the family in Illinois. They moved into a rented cottage on an estate close to where Jean lived. They could help Jean with her growing family and be closer to the rest of the family. As usual Mum & Dad worked miracles with the furnishing of the cottage and the garden and it was a lovely home.

When Mum died of breast cancer in 2011 Dad moved into a small care flat in Chesterton. Being a former boarding school boy he always made the best of things and never complained about anything. He got into a routine of visiting Jean, walking, reading, going for coffee and lemon drizzle cake at the shop on the corner.

St Josephs, Michigan 2015. Dad had a minor stroke in California and another one when he was in Indiana. It was decided he should move to a small care flat in St Josephs as Jean was no longer in Chesterton. She had moved to Bristol, Indiana following her divorce to Philip. Doug and family lived in St Josephs.

Summary. Although this may sound like the rise and tragic fall of a family there have been happy times along the way. There have been home improvement projects that became happy family homes. There is a large new generation of the McClain family. This one has not grown up in a privileged environment. They have learnt some humility from their experience.

Chapter 7 Chicago early 1970s

In 1974 I completed my schooling at Chicago High. I was a middle of the road student in terms of academic, sports, and popularity. I didn't find school or teachers very inspiring and had been a bit of a rebel without wishing to draw to much attention to myself. For some reason I was regularly getting into trouble and still do. I think it was someone's way of letting me understand things from all points of view. I also had a bit of a chip on my shoulder and inverted snobbery in my DNA. This could go back to my early days growing up in the rebellious 60's or awareness of the injustice that went on in the 70's in Chicago when industry was decimated. I would have liked to be a working class hero, but I was middle class, so I was a rebel without a cause. Many of my friends were the same but were saved from going the whole hog by their skill and intellect. Quite a few of them are now successful attorneys, doctors, and more. The previous two or three generations of McClain's were farmers, officers in the forces or professionals. I was on a different path. If I had known how difficult it would be I probably would not have. I ignored the advantages that private education and my background gave me. I went for jobs that most people from my background would not. I would do farm work, dismantling closed down industrial buildings and construction. I did a lot of different things that brought in a bit of money then, but didn't lead anywhere. I learned that people didn't always pay you for what you did. I also learned that blue collar look after their own, if their lucky. They don't do guys like me any favors or respect. When I left school I had a devil may care attitude about the future. I was enjoying my freedom from being institutionalised at school. I was driving around the countryside in beat up cars with my pals, visiting as many bars as possible, playing pool. When my clever friends started going to university it came as a bit of a surprise to me and I felt I ought to do a bit of further education. Dad would have liked me to be a vet like him. People often say "why didn't I" which irritated me. I ended up doing architecture at the local college. I tried but my heart wasn't in it. After 2 years scraping by at college I did a year out at an old fashioned firm of in Boston as an apprentice on a ridiculously low salary. I did it and scraped by but it wasn't very inspiring. During this time I had to get accommodation. I answered an ad for a flat share and went to view a place at Back Bay in Boston. A girl called Shania who was about my age had a room there. She was studying psychology. It was in a good central area close to my work in the city. At the time my old friend from Chicago, Doug Jones was working in Boston getting some experience in a department store before going into the family firm Jones & Horner. So was his brother John. He already had a circle of friends in Boston that met in a pub maybe called the Worlds End nearby. Shania joined the circle. Things moved quickly and Doug fell in love with Shania and moved in with her. If I wasn't such a dope I shouldn't have let that happen and made the move first. I was still very inexperienced with women. I was finding it a bit of a struggle to keep up with the social scene as they seemed to be out most nights and I had very little money. There was a girl called Fenella at my firm that I liked but my inexperience screwed that chance. My friend Charlie from college days did better I think. I had spent some time in a grotty flat in Chicago with him Roddy & Graeme who sadly died at 21 due to our excessive lifestyle. He choked on vomit after a heavy drinking session. Unknown to anyone he was starting to suffer from epilepsy. This was a tragic loss and a hard lesson for young men. I went back to Chicago at the end of my experience. I decided not to go back to architecture and do other things. After a few temp agency jobs I got a job in the buff shop at furniture makers who made wooden bar furniture from raw wood. It was a machining joiner shop, very traditional, fixed hours, union shop. My job was probably the worst. I had to sand every component on a variety of machines to make it fit and smooth. It was a hard job to learn because you had to turn components with your finger tips on a revolving sandpaper belt. If you were not careful you would sand the ends of your fingers till they bled. You could not work with bloody or taped fingers. You would also incur the wrath of Davey for being too slow. Nobody wanted this job. Davey, who nobody liked, was difficult to get on with. I think he liked me more than the rest because he was after my ass! I stuck that out for the best part of a year. The money was good by my standards at the time. It paid for my pub lifestyle in Lincoln Park. By now I had an old green Volvo I drove around in. I was having a drink with my friend Al (Spoon) in the Ship Inn.

Me: I fancy a change. I have got the summer holiday coming. I think I will go West and try my luck. Where do you think I should go? At the time I was not well travelled.

Spoon: Looking behind the bar there was one of those racks of peanuts where the more peanut packs you removed the more of a winsome models breasts were exposed in a scene from San Francisco. I had passed through San Francisco when I was little after a long journey in the back of Dads car going to his younger brother's wedding in California. I could remember driving over the Golden Gate Bridge. It was clear in my memory. Suspension bridges were part of my DNA. The idea appealed to me.

Me: San Francisco it is then. I have got some holiday pay coming to me. That's it. We raised a glass.

Chapter 8 San Francisco late 1970s

It was 1975, I was 20 years old. I handed in my notice to coincide with the trade summer holiday, got my holiday pay. I said my farewells to friends and family. Packed the Volvo with my few possessions and headed west to an unknown future. Some would say it was a rash move. At that time in USA if you didn't have a profession to pursue the prospects were not good. So bad that some of my generation committed suicide young. I had no contacts there at all. I took Route 80 West for more than 2000 miles with motel stops at Waverley Nebraska, Evanston Wyoming and Reno Nevada. It's a long, long way. I have always held a view that you don't adapt to your surroundings if you fly. By land you adapt to your surroundings and appreciate the journey. When I got close to San Francisco I stopped in Strawberry. I thought the name was funny but what was happening that day was even funnier. Strawberry as I remember is an old fashioned main street with quite a lot of pubs on a wide straight road up a hill. That day when I parked one side of the road and pubs was full of people dressed as English and American troops from the American War of Independence. The other side was full of Harley Davidsons parked up and the massed ranks of the Hells Angels. It turned out that each group had decided to gather there the same day. In my vivid imagination there would be a mass brawl on the street between the two groups. I spent most of my life to date in and around Chicago. This was interesting. The California scene was warm, colourful and inspiring. I stayed for the afternoon and witnessed the troops doing a battle enactment in an adjoining field, complete with muskets and cannons that fired. The Hells Angels were quite a sight. Previously I had only read about them or in "Easy Rider" but this lot definitely looked the part and scary. They drank, postured and gunned their Hogs up and down the street but there was no violence. I continued my journey into San Francisco across the magnificent Golden Gate and stopped on Richardson Avenue near the Polish Church. This stretch of road was to become part of McClain history but I didn't know it then. Looking around me I could see that Elvis and Eric Clapton were playing at the Cow Palace in town this year. There was a big fire work display to celebrate 4 July Independence Day at the Golden Gate. I was parked opposite an entrance opposite with a sign above reading GJ Construction. I took a deep breath and went to their reception. I was introduced to one of the bosses Gavin Rae and told him who I was, where I was from, and what I had done. Well I was amazed when he said I could have a start. I was used to rejection by now in Chicago.

I drove to Leavenworth where I found the Shiy Yu-Lang Central YMCA. I booked in there to tide me over. It wasn't very pleasant. Everything was very basic. There were a lot of homeless people there and screams at night. Somebody told me to put the bed legs on my shoes or they would surely be gone by morning. Any way it was cheap and I wouldn't stay long. Guys at work told me to check the Chronicle for rented accommodation. Chinatown at the time had lots of rented places where hippies and Irish stayed while working in and around the city. At the time pubs in the area would have groups of Irish construction workers drinking Guinness at the bar after work. Soon I saw an advert for a bedsit I could afford at Grant Avenue. Jim and Neil, the landlords, a gay couple, had the basement. I took the place on the 1st floor as it was close to the yard and affordable.

I started work as a labourer on a refurbishment of a rank of homes on the corner of Alma Road and Whiteladies Road in San Francisco. GJ Construction had all their own men. We were issued with overalls with GJ Construction written on them according to trade.

Blue, labourers, ground workers, carpenters, electricians, plumbers

Tan, Plasterers,

Brown, bricklayers

White, Painters

Most of the men had done apprenticeships. There were quite a few families in the firm. As a labourer my work involved material handling, fetching and carrying by wheel barrow, demolition, cleaning, excavating, foundations, forming openings. From there I progressed to working specifically with ground workers on foundations, drainage & slabs. Then I was with bricklayers. Fetching and carrying for them. Building walls, repairing stone, and forming openings. Then I was with plasterers. Fetching and carrying, plaster boarding, and mixing up for plastering & rendering. I kept an eye on the carpenters and I liked the work they were doing. I asked how I could get into that. Some of them said they had done their apprenticeship straight from school but I was a few years too old for that. Others said they had been on a six month GTS Government Training Scheme. Stan Buck the other co-director of GJ was on the board of the scheme and took them on. I worked for quite some time as I was and gained good experience labouring on the trades I mentioned. I worked with Irish Bill the Ground worker who drank gallons of water because he had a kidney stone. Trev who had some odd tattoos including a teardrop under one eye. I learned that boys who had been in a young offender's institution chose this tattoo. It symbolised the tears of being locked up. Bill the Bricklayer, like Superman, Catweazle the Kiwi, another Bill, Ivor the Engine from Wales, Charlie the Plasterer, Bill Glasgow in the joiner shop and many others. I hooked up with some of them at weekends to do private jobs or "foreigners". One of these is memorable. We extended and put in a floor slab on an antique shop across the road from the Alma Road job. Bill & Ben the brickies, Catweazle, and I on the strength of doing that job got asked to look at some work at the owner's home in Portola Valley. He wanted his 2 storey attic bungalow extending by cutting and filling the hillside it was on to form a large garage. He confided in Bill and showed him plans he had drawn up for a fallout/earthquake shelter beneath the garage. At the time people were worried we were going to be nuked in the cold war and such things were not uncommon but it had to be a secret. By the time I saw the job a great cut had been taken out of the side of the hill. The house foundations were exposed. The foundations for the retaining walls were ready to go. Bill had been working there in the evenings. He fancied himself as a bit of a superhod and looked it. Me and Catweazle went there at the weekends only when we were not busy at Alma Road. Transport was an old Dodge pickup and a trailer which was common for builders on a foreigner at the time. It soon became apparent that something was going on. Bill would disappear into the house to look at the plans and would be away for quite some time. One Saturday morning the owner roared up in his Jaguar and rushed into the house where Bill was. We looked at each other. It was a poor secret that Bill was fucking the owner's wife and he was here to catch them at it. Ben told us to tidy up, pack up, we were off. Sure enough Bill soon appeared jumped in the back and off we went. We never went back and we heard that things stayed just as they were for quite some time. There was a bad earthquake that year. It rained considerably, the clay expanded and shrunk and the house started to fall into the foundations. Bill who had a wife and 2 small children never let anything faze him. He was soon back to his old self laying bricks, singing at the top of his voice in proper western style, and flexing his muscles. We retreated to the Smugglers Cove to lick our wounds. As I said I went to San Francisco with no contacts but I soon met people. At my bedsit at Grant Avenue I met Ray Bickle who had the bedsit upstairs from me. Ray was my age. He was currently an electrician changing light bulbs on the Golden Gate. Cool job. He had been having a hard time. His mum and dad had died recently and he was finding it hard moving from the tough suburbs where he had lived with his family to bedsit land. He also had his dog Scamp, a ginger collie type thing with him which was not ideal on your own. Ron said he met some friends at the Old England pub in Chinatown so I went along. The Old England wasn't far but you probably wouldn't find it if you hadn't been taken there. It was tucked away in a dead end street by a doctor's surgery. It was basically a rambling detached house with sprawling terraced gardens round about. A large man called Morris and his wife and family ran the place. It had an eclectic mix of clientele. Chinatown I got to know was a part of Frisco full of character, good, bad, and interesting. You would get all kind of people in there, Irish ground workers, hippies living in squats or vans, black Jamaicans form the hood, artists, musicians, dossers, eccentrics. It was a great place for people watching. It was a very busy place. Booze was much cheaper then. 50 cents a pint and we thought that was a lot. Through Ray I met Art Moore, Jelly Bean, Steve, Sean, Nick Roy, Len, and many more that were all my age. I immediately fitted in with this crowd which is strange because back home I would never have fitted in with a crowd from the South side of Chicago. I would immediately be labelled as a toff from the High school and them a gang of hoods. It was different here. We didn't know each other. Had no pre conceived idea's. I was just like them, a young man, finding his feet in adulthood. They didn't know or care where I was from. What I liked about the lads was they didn't have the kind of attitude I was used to from lads from their background back home. In the Old England there is stairs beside the bar that goes upstairs to another large bar with 2 pool tables and doors out to a large beer garden. I would spend a lot of time here for the next few years. There were juke boxes on each level and the Old England at the time had a great mix of reggae, ska, and rock. Part of the reason for the mix of people at the Old England it was the frontier between white Frisco and diverse Chinatown and people would meet there to meet their "man" to purchase their drug of choice. We were not into drugs but it was a bit of a scene and we were on the fringe. Playing pool was very popular. If you won your game you stayed on the table. The challenger would put 50 cents on the table and their initials on the blackboard. Once I was established I prided myself on staying on the table for 2 hours. I lost my place on the table when I had too much to drink. So it was a heady mix of music, pool, boozing, and interesting people coming and going. They had another garden at the back with 2 baseball nets where it is said Mike McCormick and Giants players practiced in the 60s. Later on I played for the Coronation Pub on the bay and we practiced there.

Chapter 9 Anthrax

1976. I was 20 years of age. In the summer of 1976 I was harvesting on farms in Illinois and Indiana. In previous summers as a student I had been on a course at the Department of Agriculture and learned some harvesting skills. We would form gangs of between 2 and 10 and hire our services out to farmers at a rate per acre or hectare. For students or young people it was thought to be good money. The rub was in my experience you weren't always paid for your hard work. Something that I got used to in life and never resolved. Anyway the long hot summer of 1976 is still talked about to this day. In my gang that year if I remember correctly was Stevie, CairNoMor, Mike. We worked on farms over a wide area of Illinois. I was staying at Mum & Dads home at Lonsdale, Indiana.

We would meet early in the morning at Lonsdale and head off to whatever farms were on our list and work a 12 hour day in the fields. Up and down we would go until we had checked the whole field. I enjoyed this job. We travelled all over the state in the best of summer weather. We were a gang of young men making good money. This particular summer it was very hot most days. It was normal for us to strip to our shorts when we were working. On at least 1 occasion we went for a paddle in a ditch at the end of the field we were working. After the season was over a spot developed on my calf which was becoming more enflamed like a bullet hole. I showed Dad and he immediately didn't like the look of it and sent me to A&E in Chicago. They confirmed that I had Anthrax. My Dad knew the signs. His work put him in contact with Anthrax. It was meant to have been isolated but wasn't. If cattle died of Anthrax they were supposed to be disposed of safely. The spores can remain in the ground and water courses for many years. I could have got the infection paddling if I had a cut. They put me into an isolation room and started pumping me full of antibiotics. This was serious and quite rare. The local press got hold of the news and were outside looking for a story. I can't remember how long I was there but I was young and fit and made a quick recovery. I left hospital with a swab bandage on thc wound that I had to change regularly. It wasn't a pretty site. Like a bullet wound eating into my leg. They told me to keep a close eye on it as it could flare up again.

The same summer we had a VIP visitor to Lonsdale. Seattle Slew the undefeated Triple Crown Winner was on a national celebrity tour of US bookmakers. He was visiting bookies in Chicago. Someone in horse circles recommended Lonsdale stables was a suitable place for him to stay on his visit. We had the pleasure of having Seattle Slew and his lads come to stay. On the evening they arrived we got him settled. He was a very friendly horse. John, Doug and I took the lads into Chicago to have a beer and get a Chinese to go. The funny thing was Seattle Slew finished off a chow mein.

1977. On my return to San Francisco my Anthrax wound flared up again and I was confined to an isolation hospital outside the city. This was a scary looking institution surrounded by a barbed wire perimeter fence. The buildings looked like a prisoner of war camp. I was in an isolation room next door to a man who had just come off a flight with Lasa fever. I realised the seriousness of my illness. I was in there for a couple of weeks being pumped full of antibiotics. An old friend Chris from Chicago by coincidence was the registrar on my ward round. It was nice to have a familiar face coming to see me. I was released and am pleased to say I have suffered no ill effects since. I returned to the city and went on the Government training scheme in Carpentry & Joinery. By now I had got to know Steve Hurt who had moved into the top bedsit at Grant Avenue. Steve had been a postman but got run over leaving the Condor Club made famous by Carol Doda, and had his arm in plaster and a sling. He and Ray both played guitar and were keen on making songs, playing and wanted to form a band. One song is engrained on my memory. Influences at the time were the Stranglers, No more heroes, Eddie & the Hotrods, He was starting a scheme in electronics at the same time as me at the same training establishment. I think Steve had a Mini and I had a Suzuki 250GT at the time. Steve and two mates were always late getting there. They were quite strict about time keeping at the training centre. He and his mates like to have a little toke of hash on route which was quite potent. I don't know how they managed. I don't think they completed the course. Anyway my course was an intensive course in Carpentry & Joinery 1st fix, 2nd fix, joists, roofing, bench joinery. We were given a set of tools and had to make a box with dovetail joints at the corners to hold the tools. It was said that we should keep it to ourselves that we had not done a full apprenticeship, dirty up the tools and not use the box when we went for a job. GTS schemes were not as good as a full apprenticeship. This was a myth as hardly any chippies have done a proper apprenticeship. After 6 months I passed and as promised I went back to work at GJ Construction as a carpenter improver. By then things were different at GJ construction. They did not have a big job running. There was competition for jobs on fewer smaller jobs. The apprentice trained chippies were slagging off the trainees to Stan Buck the boss. I was and still am a bit naive about the politics of the workplace and how nasty colleagues can be. I was working on an Associated Dairies site (became ASDA) doing skirting, architrave, hanging doors in the offices. I would often jump in the van and go to the builder's yard to collect materials & plant. It was my way to help the job along. I would help other trades loading out as I did before I was a chippie. Some of the family men, who only cared for themselves, told the boss I was too slow. I got paid off. I took this really badly at the time. Still do. I wish I could have foreseen this and done something. On reflection if there is not much work and you're not a favourite you are always vulnerable. Best not dwell on it. Move on. Experience has taught me it is usually for the better. Our paths would cross again much later. On one of my regular trips home to Chicago I celebrated my 21st birthday at The Ship on the river. My friends The Prof, Tommy Mac, Spoon, Jock and more had been regulars there for the last 3 years. This was not all to the liking of the boss Crichton. Our money in the till was good, but sometimes towards the end of an evening, when spirits were high, it would get messy. On my birthday it was very messy and I got thrown in the river. I also met up with my old friend Shania from Dean Street, Boston who had moved to Chicago planning to marry Doug Jones. They were not wed. I met her at her flat off E 73rd. She was very pleased to see me. We had not got together before. It would have been difficult, better late than never. Soon after I returned to San Francisco to find she had left me something to remember her by. Later I found that I wasn't the only one of my friends to have an affectionate liaison with Shania. I was a bit put out by this but I still remember her with affection. I believe she stayed in the area and asked for me when she visited Dad at the surgery with her cat.

Chapter 10 San Francisco carpenter

1978 After a spell of doubting my abilities and thoughts of retribution. I decided it was time to get back in the saddle. I dirtied up my tools. I bought some new tools. I dirtied them up. I got an old tool bag. Practiced my story of being a time served carpenter and prepared myself for entering a brave new world via the job agencies. Work was scarce at the time so I was pleased when I got a start with Snook who seemed to have procured several large commercial refurbishments in the City centre. Looking back I can see that in the construction industry the cheapest contractor generally wins the work. The cheapest is generally the one who doesn't know what they are doing, or are desperate for turnover at any cost. Generally later rather than sooner this materialises and they go into liquidation. Anyway I have made a precarious living working for desperate contractors trying to survive in a recession. When I was young I blamed myself when it ended. I have learned not to. It got me work because they didn't enquire too closely about my background and my hourly rate was slightly lower than an old hand. The work was on listed buildings in the City. Buildings formerly owned by the Telephone Exchange that were to be done up and let out. It was a big challenge. These were big jobs with facades retained. We built new roofs, fixed new steelwork, new joists and floors, replaced hardwood doors, skirting, architraves, and panelling. Lots of restoration work. I was out of my depth but so were others. We stuck with it and the work kept going. We got paid cash in an envelope on a Friday at lunchtime. Once we got our pay no more work was done. We would all go to the pub. I remember on one occasion being in what was O'Neills on a good lunchtime session. I got in conversation with a curly haired girl of my age who worked on the trollybus. She came back to my bedsit where we spent a very pleasant afternoon. She left in the evening to go home to her boyfriend and I went down to the Old England to meet the lads. My pool wasn't up to much that evening. We were in the habit of going on from there to Keystone Korner for live reggae & ska bands, Jamaican lager or to the Cow Palace for live rock, heavy metal or Winterland

1979. It became harder to get work. I can remember winter being cold and working on the roof. It was freezing when you first went up in the morning. Everything was icy, slippery, and cold to the touch. The hours before the 10 o'clock break were hard. There was talk that Snook were not in a secure place. Men were getting paid off. I was paid off. I picked up other jobs through the agency in the city centre. I saw an advert in the Chronicle. A job agency was looking for carpenters to go to South Africa. Going to South Africa & Germany was the thing for men to do at the time. The economy was not in good shape and many took the view the rates were not worth working for here and it was better to go abroad. "Auf Weidersein Pet" with Jimmy Nail was a comedy on TV made about the period. Also Ricky Tomlinson in his book talks about black listing of union men in construction at the time. Anyway I applied for this job and to my amazement got an invitation to go for a trade test at the BRE Building Research Establishment. I was worried that my limited skills would let me down. They were looking for shuttering carpenters which I had done a little of. Shuttering carpenters make the moulds of ply and timber to pour concrete in. It is also called formwork or temporary works. On the morning of the test there were twenty of us there. They issued us drawings and instructions to build shuttering for 2 columns and a beam across the top to a reduced scale in a set time. No power tools. I found it difficult and when we were told time was up I had not finished. I looked around I could see some were better, more advanced than mine. Some were not. Some walked out at the start. We didn't get marked there and then. I left furious and hot thinking; that will be the last I will hear, and continued to beat myself up for some time. Later I got a letter from the agency. I was opening it thinking it would be the usual thankyou…sorry…unsuccessful letter. It said pleased to inform you… like you to travel to Johannesburg, South Africa to take up position of shuttering charge hand on 1 year contract etc. Find enclosed return business class ticket. Well.

Chapter 11 South Africa

1980. I flew to Johannesburg Business Class on a jumbo jet, a 15 hour flight. We had been advised prior to leaving US that the 16 to 18 of us would be working together on large projects in Johannesburg. We were working for a company called LTA Construction the largest construction company in South Africa. On arrival we were told we were going to work in the Transvaal, 100 miles up a new motorway they were building to the North. We would travel as a group and be allocated our work when we got there. We were travelling on the A road and we could see them building the new motorway as we travelled. Sometimes we could see a motorway bridge being constructed in the distance. They appeared to be building the bridges before they built the motorway. I noticed one bridge with men scrambling all over it with hydraulic breakers breaking down the concrete. I asked what was happening. The driver explained that one was wrong or in the wrong place and was being broken down. He said with a big smile that sometimes LTA stood for "Let's Try Again"! We went to LTA Office in Middleburg and were introduced to some of the personnel that worked there. We were told that a large portion of the work from that office was on SASOL plants. That is, making coal into oil. There was also work on motorway bridges. They asked us to decide amongst ourselves who was going where. Many of the group had known each other previously or formed bonds on route. They had a meeting between themselves and decided they wanted to stay together in the accommodation camp at the SASOL Plant. Me and Geordie John drew the short straw and were to go together as charge hands building a motorway bridge. That night we would stay at 2 young Afrikaans surveyor's house they had been allocated by the company. In the morning we would be shown the site by a tough Afrikaans Section Foreman we had met and given what they called a

Backy; A Mazda pickup and a trailer to stay in. We would park the trailer at a nearby dam. It was common for white workers working away from home to live on trailer parks by a lake and fish and barbeque in the evenings. This was a time of apartheid. Nelson Mandela was still in prison on Ellis Island. That evening we went to the surveyor's place. It was a nice modern 3 bed house in a good part of town. The surveyors had a VW GTI and were about our age. They were charming confident good looking blond Afrikaners. They had a circle of friends where they lived. They enjoyed a nice lifestyle barbequing most evenings. They call a barbeque "brai". The supermarkets were well stocked with lovely steaks and prawns; washed down with Castle lager and cane, (white rum) & coke. This was the staple diet. They also went to drive in movies on the edge of town. It was like an American small town lifestyle. Some girls would join them in the evenings. They were blonde good looking, and confident. My buddy and I were impressed with this lifestyle. We were probably hoping to ourselves that this lifestyle would soon be ours. As the week progressed we were shown around by the Section Foreman and we made the transition from the lifestyle we liked to working. We collected the backy and trailer and established ourselves at "the dam" which was quite a way from town. The Section Foreman looked after several sites on this stretch of the motorway so he would just be visiting. He pointed out to us that there was a pistol in a holster under the seat of the backy for our safety. He would give us the day to do our shopping then pick us up in the morning to see the site and meet the men. The following day we met up at the office. He told us to follow him to the "township" where we would pick up some men and then go to the site. We had heard of townships. Driven past them and seen them on TV. Now we were going in. He drove in on unmade roads through the basic shanty town with few facilities amongst the black Zulus many of whom were wrapped in checked or tartan rugs to ward off the morning chill. They gave us surly not welcoming looks as we went in and pulled up at a junction where a group were standing. The boss got out in a self-assured manner and started greeting the men not in a friendly way but in an "I'm the boss" kind of way. After a few curt introductions, the men were eying us with suspicion and comments amongst themselves. The foreman told them to get in the backy. They were taking their time and talking amongst themselves. The foreman got annoyed and started raising his voice to them. He told them to get a move on; sit down, shut up, kafirs; which is an insult. When they weren't quick enough he started pushing, punching, them and shouting at them till they sat meekly in the back. We were of course not used to this and felt scared, alarmed, embarrassed but tried not to show it. We were few and they were many including bystanders. Boss explained not to take any shit from the boys or they will walk all over us. You are their boss. Make sure they know it. Fuck! This is really hard-core. Are we going to be up to it? Many questions were now being raised. It was becoming apparent that we were in a sink or swim situation. We were sharp end charge hands. Most of the people we had met at the office distanced themselves from this work and we had been brought in to do it. We drove along dusty unmade roads to the site. It consisted of 2 tin round houses between 2 or 3 scrubby trees each inhabited by 20 men. The men lived so far from site they stayed for 2 or 3 weeks at a time. They would go home for a long weekend to see family and friends. They were Zulus and we were not Michael Caine and Richard Baker from the film. We knew what they had done to the British Army at Rourke's Drift in the Transvaal. Apart from the huts there was a primitive concrete batching plant. Heaps of sand, aggregate, cement, some sort of pulley shovel thing, a basic site hut and a few trenches with reinforcing started for foundations. A few introductions were made, surly responses; a bit more posturing by the foreman, drawings exchanged and before long he was off and we were on our own. The boys carried on with what they were doing with a few glances our way from time to time. We were looking at each other thinking; how would we do this. We decided we would do as we would back home and see what happened. John was a beefy bloke with a beard and could easily pass for an Afrikaner. He was quite tough and an able chippie. I always figured he'd be alright in the Wild West that was our South Africa. Me however, the middle class softy blagging it in this tough new world had better man up quick. We decided to tough it out and show them who was boss. Initially we played it like the Section Foreman Pieter. It soon became apparent that if we were like this they would carry on in a surly unhelpful way. We would feel a bit isolated working together but not involving them. We started watching them and asking them what they were doing. It wasn't easy adapting our English so they could understand. We stuck at it. Humour helped a lot. They laughed at our mistakes and we laughed. We didn't hit them. They started to show us skills they had. We sang silly songs. We gave each other nicknames. Spaniel, Daniel, Michael Jackson, We asked them what they had for breakfast, Jagula; a cheap alcoholic porridge drink in a carton that got them going through the morning chill. It always surprised us that it was cold and there was frost on the ply IN AFRICA. They asked us about the USA and UK and of course they knew things, Hollywood, Kennedy, Manchester United, Bobby Charlton, the Queen. So we muddled along. We read the drawings pretending we were telling them what to do. Reinforcing was set, shuttering was built, they showed us their way, gave us tips, how to make a drill bit from a nail. Some helped. Some didn't. I was working with one man holding a metal pin while he drove it into the ground with a sledge hammer. He missed and split my finger. I had to justifiably discipline him Afrikaans style. It didn't come easy but these incidents were rare. Shutters for columns were built, concrete was poured. It was all done using pulley systems and manpower. Sometimes if required we would go to the SASOL plant at Witbank and help there. We learnt when we went there how the others were getting on. There was some unhappiness in the camp. Apartheid was working on many levels. The blacks, the workforce were being abused by the Afrikaners mainly. There was a big neon sign above the gate telling visitors how many hours had been worked on site without a death. This did not include the blacks who regularly fell off cooling towers being built and other risky business. There was tribe warfare.There was Asians. The Afrikaans had effectively detached themselves from the workforce by hiring the likes of us. They were doing well paid jobs cruising around in a backy, supervising. Overseeing from the office and generally spreading the love. Some of the lads were militant northerners from UK and didn't like this. Some had already gone home using their return ticket. Some had decided to go home but had spoken about it too much. They were arrested and brought back to work for breach of contract. The rest of us carried on dreaming we would eventually achieve better positions. We knew there was a recession back home and we were probably better off here. When we were at the SASOL plant we would muck in with the others; fixing shuttering for floor slabs. The boys did the pour which would take to the end of the day. They would leave 2 or 3 boys with the wet concrete all night, trowelling it to a good finish. Sometimes when we wanted a change from barbequing at the dam we would go to Middleburg or Witbank. These were like the Wild West frontier towns. Not much more than 1 street with hotel bars with verandas. The bar we used in Middleburg was quite basic. Everything was fixed to the floor to avoid being thrown about. Blacks were not allowed to drink there but they served behind the bar. There was a sign behind the bar, "Customers will not be jumping over the bar and assaulting the bar staff." We were in there on one occasion watching South Africa v Ireland. Rugby was big in these towns. Especially amongst the Afrikaans who thought they were superior at most things, especially rugby. They could be quite intimidating. They were on a bigger scale than us. Probably due to all the steak they ate. They could be arrogant. As the game progressed we were supporting Ireland. Against all the odds they won. The guys in the bar weren't happy. They were drunk as well and itching for a fight. We decided it was best we leave. We had to rapidly get out of town. We were on foot with them in pursuit. Whites do not walk in South Africa. We did and attracted a lot of looks when we did. We made our way on foot back to the dam which was probably not wise. We did not know the rules. The blacks can be a threat. The Afrikaans can be a threat. Everyone is wary of everyone. There are knifes, machetes, guns, dogs to take into account. The police there tend to allow a respectable time for incidents to sort themselves out before making an appearance. On the way back we had to skirt round outlying homes. A vicious looking Alsatian came running towards us barking. We decided the safest place was in an empty swimming pool nearby. The owner called his dog back and we carried on our way. On another occasion in Middleburg, I was walking up the covered sidewalk. 3 large boys were walking towards me. The custom at the time was for the boys to step aside and let the master by. On this occasion they didn't and I had to give way. The times, they were a changing. When we got cabin fever we would make the 100 mile drive to Johannesburg. We were advised to be careful what we did there because it was a dangerous place. The police could be harsh. We had not had any female company in the sticks. We heard there was night clubs in Johannesburg. These night clubs were strictly speaking illegal. They were mixed race. They were left alone by the police so long as there was no trouble. We had a taxi driver take us to an address we had been given. We got in. The place was a sprawling, sumptuous, bordello, richly furnished and dimly lit. It had several bars. It was full of every race and creed enjoying life as it should be. The women were gorgeous. It had the feel of a brothel. We were all keen to have some fun. We spent a very pleasant evening there. The word went round that the police were on their way. We had to make a rapid exit and find a taxi. One of my regrets about South Africa is that I did not get the chance to be a tourist. I did not see the Kruger Park and all the wild life. I did not get to Cape Town and the coast. We were workers. My colleague's aims were to make money and go home. I think my buddy would fit in and stay. I got a fever and had to stay at home in the trailer. I had a flu virus. I had time to reflect. Most of the guys I had come out with had gone. Some had been picked up and returned to site. I found it difficult to relax in this environment. I wasn't happy with the politics and the insecurity. It was very different to life back home. You had to fend for yourself. No benefit in calling the police if something went wrong. I decided to quietly take my leave and go home. The fact I was ill would give me the chance to get on a plane. I would be gone before they knew it. The other difficulty was taking money out of South Africa. We had heard the others had converted there earnings into gold Kruger ands. They hid them in their toolbox. They planned to retrieve them when the box was freighted home. This was very risky. As often as not, the box would be stolen, before it got on the plane. I was able to be quick and discreet enough to get on a jumbo jet with a few possessions (for some reason 1 sock only.) The flight home again 15 hours was eventful in that I was in business class with free drinks. I got drunk and felt sick. I got in a que for the toilet but unfortunately didn't make it before I was sick.

Chapter 12 College San Francisco

I went home to Lonsdale, Indiana and had a bit of a meltdown. I suppose I had eventually had to face up to the fact that I am not as strong, able, and brave as I would like to be. So much for the working class hero. You are what you are!

1981 City College, San Francisco. I spent the summer in Indiana then returned to Frisco in a VW Beetle I had purchased. 3 days driving and 2 motel stops in Kansas and Utah. I had enrolled at City College to complete my Construction degree. I rented a room nearby in Chinatown. I was a bit older than some in my class as I had a chequered career to date and to follow! There was however some older than me. There were also several foreign students from Iran, Middle East & Nigeria. During enrolment we each had to tell the class something about ourselves. The lecturer joked to the class "McClain the Chicago mobster." This stayed with me for the duration of my course. They were a good bunch in my class and I enjoyed it more there than the dour institutions that were my previous experience. I think I did better because I liked it. I had experience on site. Lecturers often asked me to give the class an insight into what actually happened on building sites. This generally started a debate about what we were learning. It was a good balanced lesson to the academic, theoretical and ideal scenario. My gang at college was Dick Bean, Billy Bremner, Andy Davis, Alex Stanish, Steve Fender, Gerry Frost. I have a photograph of them all looking down on me as I sit writing at my desk. There was a lot of joking and winding up went on in lectures to spice it up. Richard Bean had a room at the bedsit in Chinatown with Steve the young bricky who had just returned from Germany and the Guru who was a hippy, lentil eating, new age cyclist who we didn't quite get but he was probably fine. I think Steve Hurd lived there for a bit. I think there was a bit of social interaction with the Old

England gang to. We spent a bit of time in the Old Ship and Biscuits & Blues. I think that was the winter there was a big snow fall in Frisco. College was suspended for a week. The snow was so deep no cars moved. We spent the week shuffling up to the bar in the few tyre tracks in the road and maintaining a diet of beer, pie and beans. Normally it was my habit to join the lads at the weekend. Art Moore now lived in North Beach. I would drive over there in my Beetle which had a broken exhaust. The tale at the time was that Art could hear me start my car in Chinatown and all the way to North Beach. It took me the best part of two years to finish my degree. For me this was a personal challenge. Most people maintain the letters after their name throughout their career. For me I have always doubted the merits of institutions. For many years as a Site Superintendent in housing it would have been seen as me being over qualified if I advertised it. Later in my career I could see its benefits. In the commercial sector the title opened up more senior roles. I take the view that if you take short cuts in climbing the ladder in construction you will be exposed. I have climbed all the mountains I want to climb in construction now. I had a few falls recently so I am not keen to go back. I digress. I met a girl called Becks during this time. She was studying to be a teacher at college. I spent the odd pleasant evening with Becks and remember her fondly. I took up swimming during this period first of all at the YMCA and then at the City College pool. For exercise I would do 50 lengths of the pool alternate lengths breast stroke, front crawl.

Chapter 13 Vermont

1982. By now it was becoming obvious to me that I was on an unorthodox path in life. Is it because I am left handed? I wish I knew. I was middle class. Most of my friends from school were by now embarked on a successful career in the law, medicine, or business. They were upwardly mobile. They could hold their head up when asked at weddings what they were doing. I could see people grimace when I told them what I had been doing. I am downwardly mobile. I am an inverted snob. My goals are personal goals. My challenges are not recognised by folk back home. I have nothing to say to impress at a wedding or funeral. I have this desire to pull myself up by my boot straps. But I'm not working class, why bother. Nobody is impressed. Not even me. I had achieved a goal of going back to being a labourer, then a tradesman, then a construction professional. It meant something to me but not anyone else. What now. I saw myself as being on a long and fruitless apprenticeship to become a Site Superintendent. Big deal! So now I had an opportunity to go to a national housebuilder Bryant Homes as a manager in there small up and coming regional office in Burlington, Vermont. I hear you say, but you gave up management to go labouring. In my world there is no path no rule that can't be broken. This is the world of the flip, flop, snakes and ladders without prizes. I went back to move on. Moving to Vermont at the time was a revelation to me, from Chicago and San Francisco. I had seen the hardship of the USA at the time. Burlington, Vermont was at the heart of one of the most prosperous areas of the US. Looking around me there was leafy suburbs, massive lovely homes with winding drives, hidden amongst trees, pines, electric gates, high walls. Lovely little towns and villages with picture post card pubs. I moved into a shared house in popular South End.

There were 2 girls in residence. I shall call them Mary & Liz for now. I was followed by Kevin, Greg, Susan, and Izzy. (I suspect all these names are not correct) We had a good mix in the house of up and coming young professionals in an up and coming area. The world was our onion. Mary worked for the local authority and liked horse riding. Her boyfriend was a Scot and lived in another similar shared house to ours nearby. Liz was a hairdresser, she drove a Citroen 2CV. She appealed to me but was a bit reserved due to being hurt in the past I think. Kevin like me was new to the area and was a graduate in IT. He was extremely tall amiable long curly haired lad from Southport. He like me couldn't believe his luck stumbling on this jewel of good fortune. He had just got a job with IBM. Susan was a bubbly smiley blond in sales for Pierre Cardin. She was a graduate, full of energy, stressed from her fast lifestyle in sales. Greg was a good looking recent graduate from Hatfield in business studies. He was from the West. He was charming with an easy smile. He had really landed on his feet. He had just got a job selling computers for a small firm in Burlington. In his 1st week his senior partner sold a second hand what they called mainframe computer to PanAm. This was a big deal. Greg accompanied him on the deal and got commission. He also got a new Ford Mustang with all the bells and whistles for his trouble. Izzy was a local girl. She was lively, tall, and good looking. She was the youngest in our house. I think she worked in a local wine bar. I worked from an office was in Burlington. It was a 4 bed detached house with cabins attached. By today's standards the office was small. Our territory stretched from the Canadian border to New York. They had 2 cost managers the senior of which was Carl Gable. He had an office upstairs which I had a desk in as his junior. Now I thought I was laid back but Carl was something else. He like most of them originated from down South. He was tall and urbane. Carl was always stylish in a wide lapel suit, flared trousers, shirt, tie, and shiny shoes. He kept his mullet hair style carefully in place at all times. He smoked long thin cigars most of the time. He was so laid back he almost melted into his executive chair. He liked to sit with the chair tipped back and his feet on the desk puffing a cigar. He never got emotional. He took everything in his stride. Maybe he was on Prozac! I would find out as time went by there was a lot of history and politics in this office.The story was that the MD Andy McKendry had been a rising star at the Head Office down South but had come here under a cloud. His wife had sadly committed suicide. He had upset some people in high places there and had been sent here to fail. He had brought all his loyal lieutenants with him the closest of whom was Carl. Fortunes changed economically and the Northern region was starting to eclipse the head office much to their dislike as it was from a much smaller base. I have to say that in time I realised that they had a better model for success in construction than I have seen since. They had a vast land bank and a loyal group of tried and tested contractors. Carl would agree annual terms with the contractors across a range of sites. This made our job as cost managers easy to manage. The contractors were comfortable and would do anything for you, no trouble. Some would say in was uncompetitive and open to corruption but it worked. I was able to swan about over a huge area and didn't have the usual small scale valuation hassles most cost managers have. We were very much the big picture orientated. We had to prepare budgets for each site involving competitive tendering of each trade and have it signed off by the North & South MDs before being put into the company mainframe system. This was the system of financial management control. This portion of the job could be a huge chore if I had not developed a way of doing it that wasn't such a chore. Time was always my enemy. I won't go into details because my methods would probably be frowned upon. We managers in the North generally thought that the company's mainframe system which they spent years developing and millions of dollars was not serving us well. This was common to many industries at the time. Efficiency of the system was something I was always looking to maximise as a young man. We had that drummed into us at college when money was tight. I was also learning about mainframes from my house sharers. My theory was that individuals could develop efficient systems on PCs much more quickly, more appropriate and at a fraction of the development cost. I spoke to Carl & Andy about this and said I could demonstrate this to them with a Mac computer that one of Andrews children had. Andrew indulged me by setting up a table with the Mac in front of his desk. From this I went on to produce the budget spreadsheets that were the basis for financial management. I am not saying I invented this but now we use PCs, laptop, tablets, and phones to do the jobs that these highly expensive and unwieldy mainframes did back in the day. Bryant Homes had a massive land bank in and around Burlington which they had astutely bought before the industry boomed. We were providing slightly up market homes for the up and coming professionals attracted to the area. Socially we would spend many evenings in the Greyhound and having barbeques in our garden with our circle of friends. Life was good. We even had a gardener called Ern. He was an old character who looked after the rambling garden. During this period I met Joy, a lovely girl who lived with her parents nearby. I was keen on her but I think she thought me not quite right for her. There was another girl called Sarah who was great fun. She worked at the office which is not always a good idea. I heard she was having an affair with one of the bosses. She was a bucksome, lusty lass and I enjoyed her company enormously. I also had my eye on Izzy, Liz and the Greyhound landlords daughter but the girls round there were quite particular and there was a lot of competition. Life was good travelling to New York, Maine, New Hampshire, and Massachusetts. I visited prime sites where we were building better and bigger homes for the new class of yuppies. Bryant's were doing very well and they bought a large property which was to become our office. There was to be expansion to new regions in and talk of me moving to open up a new office. I had noticed that all the established staff lived in nice detached Bryant Homes which they had purchased from the company at a favourable rate. I heard grumblings from them that they were paid at Southern rates living in this expensive area. I know I wasn't paid what I would like. I was still single and not ready to settle down. There was a lot of talk about the building boom in New York and this was getting my attention more than the good life I had. I was beginning to find it repetitive. I applied for a job with Brosley Estates in Manhattan. They had a lot of land on brownfield sites they wanted to develop in New York. They wanted a cost manager to join their small team in an office in the city. I would be looking after a large new development. Anyway I got the job and gave my notice to Bryant. They tried to persuade me otherwise but I had made up my mind. It didn't help that I wrote off a company car just before I left. Looking back, leaving Bryant could be read as a huge mistake. Everyone I knew from that office did very well and became top directors and the value of their properties went through the roof. However they were taken over by Taylor Woodrow. Anyway never look back. God has a plan. When I left, to begin with I commuted from Vermont to New York. This was a hell of a commute. It was five and a half hours by car or an hour and a half flight. I would go down for the week and return to Vermont at the weekend.

Chapter 14 Manhattan

1984. I shared an office with Senior Cost Manager Pat Walts and another surveyor Mac. I was Cost Manager for South Quay, there new flagship project. Pat and Mac were looking after some existing sites in Surrey Docks and Greenwich. Pat and Mac commuted in from New Jersey. I think Pat and Mac had their hands full dealing with the sites they had. Time would show that dealing with contractors in New York was a totally different ball game to the green fields of Vermont. I think Pat and Mac had their nose put out that I had the flagship site but they knew they were struggling to keep their head above water with what they had. There was a great deal of complexity to South Quay. The system was similar to Bryant. There was dedicated software for financial management control on a mainframe computer in Brosly head office. I had to produce a budget spreadsheet backed up by competitive tendering for the project. This had to be approved and signed off by my senior, the region CEO and the national CEO before the job could proceed. The difficulty is finding a minimum of 3 contractors prepared to provide an accurate fixed price for such a complex job. I had learned how to get round this but my methods were open to criticism. I was able to produce this massive complex document in the short timescale I had and have it signed off. That was relatively straight forward compared to the day to day duties of a manager on that site. There was definitely underhand tactics involved in who got the contracts on the job and why. Many of the contractors there had got the job by their influence over people senior to me. I never found out if that was my boss and friend Pat or more likely the regional CEO. The contractors involved in these large jobs on the waterfront were in a culture of backhanders, holidays and gifts to get the job. Intimidation, threats, backhanders, gifts, holidays, entertainment to ensure their weekly, monthly, and final accounts were paid to their liking. We managers were regularly intimidated by burly gangsters if we didn't agree with their dodgy valuations. It would be a much easier life to fall in with them. I had an office on site and groups of three burly enforcers of the bricklaying contractor regularly filled my door. Charming initially offering favours, trips to football, boxing bouts. They were part of boxing culture in the city. They could turn nasty very quickly if you queried the claim. The straighter you were the more they turned up unannounced to intimidate you. They would do things like turn on you sharply as if to hit you then all laugh. Talk about taking you for a ride down river. Talk about men who came to a sorry end wearing concrete boots in the bottom of the river. This sort of talk was common. I was straight and relied on stealth, charm and lies to keep me out of trouble. A lot of my time was spent avoiding trouble. In the office I started a joke that if we were expecting a difficult customer such as the scaffolder's boss or the bricklayer's boss we should wear our security jumpers. There was no escape from our office. There was just one way in and out. We had seen these characters lift colleagues including the CEO up by the throat until their feet were off the ground. Hold them like this against the wall and demand cash for an overdue valuation. I know for a fact that some of these local gangsters went on to become some of our largest national contractors. I used to commute to work in a Ford pickup with the company logo on the side. I gave a friend of Greg, Alex a lift in to Manhattan where he was doing a work placement as part of his education. To pass the time we would make up crazy plays on a Dictaphone I had for work. Our mutual friends being all the characters and we would exaggerate their traits and things we were jealous of to the max. At the time it seemed hilarious and the journey went quickly. The Site Manager at South Quay became a friend. Noel Cahill had a look of Charles Bronson, dark hair, slit eyes and a bushy moustache. He took everything in his stride and never let things ruffle him. He was probably going along with the contractors. He bought a nice town house on the site. If you could lay your hands on a local rent book you could acquire a house at a reduced price. A lot of changing of hands of rent books was done in the nearby pub, Town of Ramsgate which we were regular visitors. The long commute was unsustainable. I had noticed that 2 sites I had visited on the waterfront had flats I could afford. I could buy a 2 bed apartment for $26,950. This was more affordable than the $75,000 homes in Vermont. The waterfront was a frontier. It was very much brownfield, reclaimed land that was swamp & industrial land. A lot of work had been done to make it habitable. It was now a massive building site. There was lots of land to develop; Lots of building going on. This was the first of the private homes. There were a few projects there. It had a reputation for being rough. A lot of people parked and lived in trailers there. Going by the vehicles and trailers they had they had plenty of disposable income. The infrastructure, the dual carriageways and roads connecting the homes had been put in first. On a Sunday the travellers would block the carriageway and hold trotting races with a lot of money changing hands in illegal betting. Eventually the police would turn up and after much debate the carriageway would open. I took out my first mortgage and went about the move to New York and all that goes with it. This was the first time I had lived on my own. I had no furnishings at all and no friends nearby. I joined a rowing club in Greenwich on the waterfront. I would go there once a week. Run around Greenwich Park. Work out in the basement with a gruelling circuit they had devised or alternatively if weather and tide was right go rowing in a 4 or an 8 on the river. I had an old friend Don Brown from school living in Upper East Side and working as an accountant. He had a girlfriend called Macey who was a journalist for a women's magazine.

PART 2 MACHER

Chapter 15 Daisy

1985. I met Daisy. This was the year I met the woman that would be my only wife, and mother of my 3 children. I was invited to the Belmont Stakes by Don. We would be watching the prestigious Triple Crown Grade 1 horse race from a prime spot on the course. In the event we did not go because the weather was atrocious. Crème Fraiche won. Instead Don invited me to a party at his garden flat. I am not much of a party animal and it was a long way across town but I went. I noticed this girl with strawberry blond hair, pink shirt, short light blue jeans, pink spotted socks and cream boots in the Dexy's style of the time. It was love at first sight. I had no doubts I had to approach her and I did. I spent the rest of the evening with her. I maybe even danced. I said to her I had another party to go to that night at the Rowing Club. Would she like to come along? She agreed so we drove all the way across town in time to catch the end of the party at the rowing club. I drove her home to her flat in New Jersey, and asked her whether she would like to come to Frisco the next day. I was going to watch the power boat racing. This was a hell of an itinerary for a weekend and involved flights. This was not usual for me but I had a feeling this was special. It turned out Daisy had been living with a previous boyfriend in New Jersey and they had split. She had not long moved into the place she shared with the landlady. To me, the neighbourhood seemed dodgy for an attractive young woman to walk around, alone. She had also not planned to go out that night but her friend persuaded her otherwise. Who was her friend? Daisy was a nanny for a family who lived by Central Park. They had 2 small children. Her husband was a trade union official. Daisy had been in Manhattan for some time. Previously she was a nanny for a family on Upper East Side. She had a network of friends who were nannies who would meet up in Central Park or over coffee looking after their charges.

She was 5 years younger than me which seemed a lot at the time. We got a flight to San Francisco and stopped at the Old Ship where we could watch the power boat racing. The lads Art, Jel, Sean, Roy were there. We didn't see so much of each other these days since I left Frisco and they were settling into homes and relationships. We had a good afternoon watching the power boats. The event would not be seen again due to deaths occurring when boats hit the harbour wall. This would be the first and last time I went to Frisco with Daisy. Looking back I'm surprised because Frisco is my second home. We never went to Malibu either. We flew back to New York. Daisy stayed at my flat that night. I gave her a ride to 9th Street station in the Greenwich Village in the morning. We were together then and Daisy moved in with me. I think we were together for a year and a half before we got married. We got engaged along the way. **10 April 1987**. We married at the First Presbyterian Church on Fifth Avenue in Greenwich Village. It was a small wedding with 4 witnesses. Don Brown, Macey, followed by lunch at nearby Claudette restaurant. There were separate functions for family in Essex and Malibu afterwards. We decided not to have a traditional wedding due to the constraints on time and budget, travel. The wedding was lovely but I had a feeling of not being in the moment due to all the things going on that I had to make sense of. Debby wore a yellow dress and we went back to the apartment via the garage where the Mustang was having work done.

Chapter 16 Leyla

Leyla was born on 12 October 1987 in Greenwich. I never had any doubts about marrying Daisy. I was in love and it always seemed a certainty. Much later demons would stalk that I did not know existed at the time. During our time together before we were married I did the Tour of the Big Apple cycle run. We visited my family and friends in California. We visited Daisy's family and friends in Essex. Daisy had an unusual upbringing as she had a sister and 3 brothers who had been taken into care. Her parents were living in a trailer when they were small. The local authority did not think this was appropriate and took the children away. Daisy and her sister were lucky in that they were fostered to the Valentinas who had children of their own. They were very active in the church. It wasn't easy for them and Daisy left to go to New York when she was quite young. Her brothers were not so lucky and whether it was because of the upbringing they had or something in them they got in trouble with the law when they were young men. Daisy it's fair to say is closer to her foster parents. Daisy and Bekka my daughters surname is Valentina. I guess it's during these visits to Essex that I sensed feelings I had not previously had. I had strong feelings to protect Daisy. They were misplaced feelings. I sometimes felt her brothers did not care for me. I can mirror this if I am not made welcome. This can become bad behaviour. Sometimes I would be in a hurry to return to New York when Debby clearly was not. I would be plainly unsociable. This was my first experience of the control and jealousy I would be accused of. I now recognise that and take responsibility for it. However I also recognise that Daisy could distance herself from my friends and family. Could this be because we were middle class and she was working class? At the time she had middle class aspirations. Or perhaps it was in reprisal for my behaviour? I didn't take much notice at the time because I was in love. At work things were changing. The Manhattan office was to be merged with the state office. The feeling in the company was that the state office was doing better than us. So there management would either replace or be senior to anyone in Manhattan. I think they thought there was some corruption. There probably was but it was inevitable in the environment and necessary to oil the wheels. My view was that building little boxes in the green fields of New York State was easier than the brownfields on the waterfront. When they arrived I soon realised they weren't the calibre of what we had. They were intent on usurping anyone who had been Manhattan Office. I was at a stage where I felt I should move forward because I felt I was doing well. I did not care who I upset. They clearly wanted to put me in my place. They insisted I drove a little Ford with the company logo on the side when they were all driving big saloons. I refused and told them I would make my own arrangements. They tried to discipline me involving human resources. I was being cast as a militant Scot. I went on holiday and when I returned they had cleared my office on site. The situation was becoming untenable. During this time I had become friendly with the foreman carpenter at South Quay, Doug Pearce. He had proved to me that he was good at what he did and managing the men. He was from New Jersey coast but lived in a trailer on site while he was working in New York. He had a wife and children in New Jersey and I know he had a girlfriend in New York. Business was booming. Subcontractors were doing very well. Circumstances were such that we had spoken about forming a company of carpentry contractors. He would look after the men on site. I would look after the money side of things. Our first job was a small site of luxury detached homes for Berkly Homes in Washington Heights. It wasn't easy but we went from small beginnings to making more contacts and more work. The big problem was nobody paid you on time.

1985 Carpentry Contractor New York. I formed a company, Midtown Building & Carpentry Ltd. We had a tiny office on 5th Avenue in Midtown. To begin with we had the job at Washington Heights with 2-4 men. I was busily pitching for more work with anyone I could think of. We did work for several big developers in the city. Our workforce grew from a few men to 20-30. It was extremely challenging to work within the price you had. Claims for additional work to the contract were always an issue. They inevitably were not paid after spending a lot of time pursuing them. I found that price work for the men did not work because the main contractor never had the job sequenced or ready sufficiently to complete stages of price work. We ended up hiring mainly Kiwi and Australian carpenters on good day work rates hoping that by working efficiently we would make a profit. The incentive was always that we had seen contractors at South Quay do very well for themselves. However they were using means of making money that I was not prepared to. I am talking about backhanders, sweeteners, using the business as a money laundering operation for criminal activities, not paying the men, tax fraud. It all went on. Not having day work paid was a huge headache and usually ended in falling out with the main contractor or developer. I began to sympathise with contractors who resorted to threats and violence to get paid. I also had an issue with my partner. I had heard that he was living the life of Riley. He was living as if we were doing better than we were. He was having fun with the young carpenters in the evening. He was also a bigamist. His authority on site was diminishing. I confronted him and eventually it was decided that he bow out and I take over everything. By **12 October 1987** when Leyla was born I was running the business. I was at Greenwich Hospital with Daisy who had gone into labour first thing in the morning. I was making phone calls to my foreman at a site on the waterfront. 2 major events were taking place the same day. Leyla was born. We had a new job starting the same day. I was making phone calls to the foreman from the hospital corridor. Looking back on these days I can scarcely believe it happened. To move, buy a home, get married, start a family, establish a demanding business in such a short space of time. It just happened and was dealt with. It wasn't planned. Many people did the same at the time, thinking it was normal. It was not. I think we were manoeuvred politically by a desire to have an economy based on a nuclear family of both parents working and paying for childcare. At the same time computerisation had been introduced to the market economy and was causing chaos. There were huge peaks, and troughs, in stocks, and interest rates. Fortunes were made and lost. For us it was like being in a stormy sea in a very small leaky boat. To herald this Leyla was born just before the **Great Storm of 1987.** This event caused a huge amount of damage to trees and property. I was back and forth to the hospital in my two tone Mustang and trying to keep in touch with what was happening on site. All around trees, scaffolds, walls, fences were down. We were now living at a 3 bed home across the road from the apartment that I had purchased for a reasonable $37,000 I think. Daisy had a job as a primary school helper round the corner. I used to look forward to the weekends when we would go to Greenwich Market. Leyla would be in a pouch strapped to my front and I would have a drink stood outside the Coach & Horses on the corner of the market while Daisy browsed the shops and stalls. I can remember walking in Greenwich Park with Leyla looking at the damage done by the storm. We would go to the Chinese restaurant. The staff would make a fuss of Leyla. They took her to the kitchen to show the kitchen staff. She was a cute baby. At work I had returned to South Quay. This time on the site next door to the one I had been manager as the carpentry contractor for the developer where they were building 250 homes. I had the contract for Phase 2. When I visited site I occasionally bumped into associates from my days as a manager there. I met a painting contractor boss who I knew and did not like as he had tried to claim more than he was due and I had disputed his claims. He was a tough enforcer type. Looking back that was how you had to be to survive. He approached me with the customary friendliness masked with a look that could kill, a crushing handshake, and a sharp turn away and turn back as if to strike followed by a fake smile. All designed to intimidate. I guess he felt terms were levelled now that I was a contractor out in the open. Not protected by working for a developer amongst colleagues in an office. He was right. This was his turf. This was an environment with many dangers and predators; People who would steal tools and equipment; Men who would lie to you about how much work they had done and claim more; Site managers looking for backhanders for having you there; Site managers having work done on "finished areas" and not paying for it; Managers trying to maintain budgets by not paying contractors. Power struggles and politics. It was all here, much more so than anywhere else in my experience. When you are young and able you think you have the tools to manage this and profit. Few do. Only the exceptional like Walt Pidgeon of Berkly Homes; Gerry Ronon of Hebron; and of course Trump. They take profit from site wars.

Chapter 17 Black Monday

19 October 1987 Black Monday. A week after the Great Storm World Stock Markets crashed. It was very real to me as I had spent several years working in the shadow of Wall Street. I had seen the development of computerised trading from the traditional means and the important development of pcs and mobile phones. I knew our bubble had burst but I found it frustrating that when I tried to talk to friends and family about it they didn't understand. You had to be there. I had lots to think about and some difficult decisions to make or I would be screwed. The effect of this took years to impact the rest of the world. By the time they noticed in Scotland I was over it. It was like a tsunami. It affected everything for years especially construction in New York. My position was I had 25 men working on the site on the waterfront. They had been carrying out work on the previous phase on the Site Managers instructions for several months in addition to the work we were contracted to do. I was not being paid for the day work despite many meetings. It was causing cash flow problems. Since Black Monday the developer had decided to slow things down due to sales and values dropping. My prices were based on the previous production rate. I tried to get a resolution but they seemed content to screw me. I decided to end it. I would pull off. I would pay off all the men and close the business. We as a family had discussed the pros and cons of living in New York. We decided it was not the best environment to bring up children as things were. We also knew that if we did not sell our home now it would lose its value over the next few years. I wanted to move to Massachusetts. Daisy agreed with me. The first thing I did was I went to the site and gathered the men together. It was Friday. I paid them. I told them I was pulling off site. I thanked them for their service. Nobody said much. I didn't get punched. Everyone knew how things were. Many of them did a deal to stay working there. I of course received no more money after that day. There followed a period of uncertainty. I was at home. I did not know who was going to turn up on the doorstep looking for payment. There were a lot of open accounts. This went on for several months till the house sale went through. I'm guessing this was a very hard time for Daisy. I didn't know what I was doing. I was trying to do things to make it better. Daisy understood even less. She was starting to hate and fear construction. It was a brutal business. It affected us more than most. Daisy kept her own council. Children and home was rightly her priority. Some of this time is a blur to me. I think I was in shock. I'd like to hear Daisy's side of it.

1989 Rockport, Massachusetts. I can't remember the details of how we moved. I bought a wreck of a house in Rockport. My Mum had noticed the ad in the local paper and said it was a nice place. We had a walk around and liked it. The house had great potential as a family home but needed loads doing. I wanted to be well located for working. I got a job as Site Manager (my original ambition) for a firm based in Boston on a hotel in Springfield. We were building a swimming pool, leisure centre extension and refurbishment of 3 floors of the hotel. I was 32 years old. I rented a flat in a poor neighbourhood. The plan was to work at the hotel and live in the flat in Springfield. I would hire contractors to do the work on the house in Rockport. Manage it myself and visit at the weekends. I can't remember how much I consulted Daisy about the plans but I felt bad about transporting her from New York to Springfield. I think she was scared but she kept her own council. I was working for IB Construction during the week. They had built a series of leisure centres for Holiday Inns around the US and this was the latest. They had an established group of contractors from Boston who would travel up and stay in the hotel. I would hire labour locally if required. The labour from Boston were well drilled professionals. The local labour could be troublesome. The managers would come to Springfield once a fortnight to see how things were going and have a project meeting. At the weekend I drove to Rockport to see how things were going on the house. I had bought a Chevy pickup and picked up materials for the work on route. I was conscious of the fact I was not spending enough time with Daisy. She was pregnant with Bekka. Thinking back this was an issue for many young men at the time. An environment existed where the conditions for a family were changing rapidly due to the politics of the nuclear family. Having to spend a lot of time away from home and travelling was the norm. Luckily Daisy met a friend through a local nursery who knew Springfield. This helped. The work progressed well. I had to put up with the local labour. In time it became apparent that most of the workforce knew each other. Many were related and lived on the same estate. Theft was an issue. It was usual for carpenters to be on price. The one I had was not up to it. The work they had done in a week did not measure much. They were not paid much. The site was vandalised over the weekend. I was threatened on occasion. I hired a local builder to look after the house at Rockport. To begin with I trusted him but as time went by my hardened instincts were beginning to doubt him. I stuck with him. Better the devil you know. The house had to be stripped back to the bare bones, propped up and substantially rebuilt.

Chapter 18 Bekka, Rockport

9 July 1989. Bekka was born in Rockport. The hotel was complete and we had moved into our new home. The move to Rockport had been difficult. I had been fully committed to the hotel job and hadn't had the time it needed to take care of the house. The builder I had hired had not made good use of the time on the house and there was a lot to do. I dispensed with his services and we moved in with an incomplete kitchen, no drainage, and plenty more. I was used to this scenario from growing up with Mum & Dad, and of course my job. Daisy was not and had two infants to think about. Traditionally it's a husband's duty to provide for his wife and family. I confidently got married and entered into this. Events had conspired to make me doubt my abilities to do so. I think by now Daisy was beginning to doubt me too. I was invited to the Opening Day of the hotel which I am guessing was after Bekka was born as I asked whether I could take Daisy and the children to the event. The day did not go well. Some of the local men were waiting in the bar to receive their final payment. The Project team and hotel management were enjoying a buffet lunch in the main meeting room. I was in an awkward position. I wanted to show Daisy the job. I wanted to enjoy the day after all the hard work. I felt it was my duty to see the men were paid. I was back and forward to my bosses to ask them politely to pay the men. They were dismissive. The men were becoming more anxious. I was getting angry. After asking a few times I told them to leave the function and pay the men in a direct way. There was a bit of an atmosphere in the room. We as a family felt we had not been made very welcome. There had been talk of me going on to other jobs but I never heard from them again.

1990 The next 5 years were probably the most important and pivotal in my life. We were in our family home, lovely wife, two lovely daughters; lovely neighbourhood; safe and secure. What could possibly go wrong? Well quite a lot actually. All I had to do was keep the money rolling in. That's the model I grew up with and wanted; Easier said than done. I had always found it difficult to get work here. I had forgotten this. I had allowed my romantic ideal of family life to bring me home. I liked the place. Massachusetts had never been good for my work. I found it difficult to fit in there. There parochial small mindedness. Most people I had to work with were working class. They did not like middle class types like me telling them what to do. Maybe I'm wrong? I didn't suffer from this in New York or San Francisco because they didn't have the right label for me. Here I got the impression there wasn't much work in the first place. What there was would be dealt out carefully to friends and family. Where did that leave me? I worked where I was needed for my particular skills and work ethic? I wasn't in the habit of going cap in hand for anything. I also wanted to spend quality time with my family when they were young. I did not want to be a father who was not there to see their children grow up. I also had a past that would catch up on me. What happened to the footloose and fancy free man of 5 years ago? Gone! I knew I loved Daisy and the children and I was determined to make it work. Something wasn't right. I was getting a lot of rejections for jobs that were poor jobs. I was becoming insular. I had my friends and family. Daisy and I shared their friendship. Daisy had her friends and family. We shared their friendships. Cracks were developing. My love for Daisy never wavered but I think she was starting to look for something outside the family. I think she was seeing a different side to me that she didn't like. This became more apparent when she was pregnant with Jim. Although we never spoke about a plan at all I was pleased to be married and having children. I was looking forward to our life as a family. When Daisy was pregnant with Jim I got the impression her enthusiasm for the future was wavering. She said Jim was 1 too many at that time. I can understand her concern given the difficulties we had been through. I had faith in our future. Things got harder. I got a job as Site Superintendent on a Doctors Surgery nearby. I was on the job for about six months. The building was substantially built and starting to be fitted out. I was not happy on the job. The firm I was working for had some direct labour. There ways were not my way. I do better with managing subcontractors than direct labour. My experience is that direct labour has too much power that they use against a new manager; Similar to player power in football. A lot of talk goes on behind your back which spreads to the project team. After a while you get the sense there is an insidious movement against you on site. It's bad for business. If it gets like this I leave. I don't believe in trying to turn the tide of discontent. I have proved myself so many times in the industry I have no desire to do it on every job I go on. Some people are just bad and not worth bothering with. Nevertheless it hurts when I can't take a job happily through to completion. It makes me not wish to attempt to do it again.

Chapter 19 Jim, Rockport

26 October 1990. Jim was born at Rockport. I was so happy to have a baby boy and I now felt our family was complete. To celebrate and demonstrate to Daisy how I felt I got a vasectomy. I remember my Dad didn't think this was a good idea. Maybe he could see the future. It was a very happy time. It was also a hard time. Times were hard economically in the construction industry. Not many people were brave or foolhardy enough to have 3 children in this climate. 3 years after we moved into our home I was facing having to sell it to pay off debts from the past. Daisy was feeling the strain of our circumstances. She was also fed up of constantly being pregnant and caring for small children. She was losing site of the woman she was. The pressures of family life led her to go out. She made new friends. We spent less time as a couple. I was able to look after the children much of the time because I was not working. My self-esteem was suffering because I couldn't get work. I became less outgoing in the village. We were no longer in the dinner party circuit. I began to feel jealous that Daisy was thriving socially while I was in decline. What I was feeling was new. It wasn't good and it was getting worse. I did not know how to deal with it. I was in denial for years. I concentrated on doing as much as I could at home without money. I don't think that helped. Daisy saw this as her domain and would rather I was out earning money. There were a lot of absentee fathers in the village. They worked away all week. They were with their children at the weekend. I was not pursuing opportunities for this reason. I can remember one afternoon coming home from work, our neighbour was in the kitchen having a coffee with Daisy. I had had a difficult day at work. Our neighbours were friends. They both had good jobs and no children. He was a regular visitor to our home as he finished earlier than me. Something in me snapped and I let him no he was no longer welcome. Of course Daisy was not happy. There were several incidents like this over the years that drove us apart. Things were getting harder for us all the time. Even government policy at the time seemed stacked against the family. Sisters were starting to do it for themselves. I felt under siege and wanted to close ranks as a family. I felt isolated. We spent 2 years going to marriage guidance. I felt that was stacked against me. The good thing about this difficult time was that I spent more time with the children. I think that was a good thing in the long run. I was with them a lot of the time during that period from 1990 to 1995. I was with them from birth till after they started attending school. I was there tending to their needs, playing in the park, going to the beach, and just being there watching them grow and learning to communicate. That has stayed with us. Many Dads in particular missed that chance I think. Families were under siege during this era. Selling our home was I think the last straw that broke Daisy's heart. We had to move into a procession of rented homes in and around Rockport. I was pretty much a broken man by now. I didn't have the confidence or the money to go out and find a new home. It was in the hands of the mum's network and I was just an inconvenient addition to the family. I was constantly being reminded by the mums of little jobs I could do round the village. Each one was a little stab in my heart. Eventually I started doing bigger jobs locally. It wasn't what I was used to and only paid enough to scrape by. My friend Doug Jones from school had moved to Rockport. We both liked to run, (it keeps your spirits up) we ran along the coastal path. I went on to do 10k, half marathons and the New York Marathon in 1997 when I was 40 years old. 3 hours 45 mins. I am finding it very hard to write about this time in my life. I keep thinking that I should never have moved back to Rockport. No good has ever come of it. We lived in a rented house up on the hill with a long garden for a while. I had a Honda car and was working for a Boston firm on a local doctor's surgery. For some reason they bought the car so when I left it sat for a long time outside our house till they came to collect it. The tyres were flat by then. A lot of time was spent in the winter keeping the stove going which was our only source of heating. What little money we had was spent on food and baby things from Walmart nearby. Daisy did a bit of child minding. I remember one day I had a row with Daisy in the kitchen because we had run up a large electricity bill on an oil filled radiator which was left on permanently for drying towels but provided little heat. Daisy obviously felt intimidated and turned round striking me just under the eye with a fish slice. The cut was bleeding. The children, including two that Daisy was looking after saw this. They probably reported back to their parents. Money isn't everything but when you don't have it you realise how difficult life can be. I started to detach myself from most of my friends from the past during this time. I felt ashamed and did not feel like keeping up appearances. I didn't want to share my time with them because we no longer had anything in common. We moved from there to a farmhouse out of town. It belonged to a family with children at school. They lived in the big house on the farm. They wanted to help us and were experiencing difficult times themselves. The rent helped. It was a relief for me to get away from Rockport as our downfall made me uncomfortable. For instance I hated going to the school gate amongst all the gossiping mothers. It was probably just in my head but that's how I felt. As I suffered Daisy was establishing a healthy network of friends in the village. Mum's network. This was making me feel worse because the relationship we once had was suffering. I was starting to feel isolated. I tried to keep these feelings down. I tried to give the children as much as we could despite the hardships. I tried enjoying simple things like time together. We had no car at the farmhouse so we were living like isolated hillbillies. Our neighbour's helped by giving Daisy and the children lifts down to school. Quite often I would run across the fields to do shopping. It was just as well I kept fit running because it was all up and down hill. I can remember a lot of good days with the children there out in the sun playing. I made a go cart which Bekka loved whizzing up and down the track on. To pass the time I cleared an old garden in front of the house that was choked with weeds. Eventually we moved from there back to a flat in Rockport. It was too small for us really. The children slept in the 2 bedrooms upstairs and Daisy and I slept on a sofa bed downstairs. It was during this time that we separated and I moved into a friend's flat in Boston. I spent my days studying computer programming and only got to see the children on visits. Thinking about it Daisy got this place when I had gone. We had already separated. We got together again after a while and things started to get better with work in the village and us attending counselling. I did a series of jobs in and around Rockport. After a while Daisy wanted to go back to work. By this time all the children were attending school. She got a job at a local call centre. This meant she would be working evenings. I didn't think much of it at the time but later it caused a problem. I was building a large extension at my friend Doug Jones house which I was finding quite demanding. I am not a tradesman. I have trade experience. I found it difficult to get good people, so often ended up doing it myself. There's the added pressure of doing work for a friend. I would have to finish early at 4pm including whatever labour was working for me and go home to look after the children for the evening so that Daisy could go to work. This went on for a while. I had grown up in a family where my Dad worked and mum looked after the home and children. This was what I was used to. This was what I wanted for us. Unfortunately with my choice of career and location it never quite worked out. The fact that I was working during the day, and looking after the children in the evenings, was making me unhappy. I spoke to Daisy about it but nothing was resolved. From my perspective Daisy seemed to have an active social life during the day when the children were at school and we never had any time together. Maybe that's what she wanted. Daisy was becoming increasingly independent. One bad day I came home in the evening tired. I'd had enough. I phoned Daisy at work and told her to come home. She did but that was effectively the end of our marriage in 1997.

Chapter 20 Divorce

What followed was a very difficult time. I thought we had a lovely family and we would be together happy ever after. I never imagined we would be torn apart and I would carry most of the blame. I had thought of myself as light hearted and easy going. But recently I had been unable to resist strong feelings coming to the fore that had broken everything apart. I had also not anticipated my inability to integrate into society and the workplace. I now found it very difficult to look at myself in the mirror and see a way forward. I knew I had to put my pride aside and provide for my children. I had to put dark thoughts aside. I had a business address in Boston. I had a house to complete in Norfolk, Massachusetts. I was staying in a trailer. The house was quite big. It was on a gap site on the edge of Norfolk. I set to work using local contractors I had worked with before. As I got to know the client I realised I was entering dangerous territory. He was reputed to be a drug dealer with a nasty reputation. I had been stung for payment many times and I was determined not to let it happen again. If he didn't pay me on time I parked outside his house till I was paid. This was a risky strategy given his reputation. The house was built in timber frame up to roof level when he contacted me to tell us to stop. He was having difficulty getting a stage payment from his bank. This worked out for me. I knew it would only be a matter of time till I got stung. I left without any intention of picking up the phone to him again. I heard from a neighbour that he and a friend came to the site one day on new Harley Davidsons. Armed cops turned up while they were on site. The cops spread them on the road and took them away. I was well out of that job. I was at a loose end with no idea what to do. Any life plans I had were in tatters. I went to California where my parents were now living. I took advantage of their attic bedroom. I needed time to try to work something out. During this time the children would fly from East to West Coast for little breaks. It wasn't easy for me or my parents being there. I was on medication for depression for the first and only time in my life. My moods were terrible. My mother suffered with depression and other health issues. Time moves very slowly in small town California if you don't have something to keep you occupied. Dad had a surgery at the house and he still had a few patients to keep him occupied at the age of 73. I thought about taking jobs, going self-employed but nothing appealed. We had the odd terrible row. I had always said that if my marriage ever got as bad as Mum & Dads I would leave because I didn't want children to grow up in an unhappy home. This is what happened but it was no better than what we had in my experience. I was trying to make sense of what happened but it always ended up with Mum in tears. There was an occasional shouting match in the back garden that could probably be heard on the street. I started to do some work on the house. It was therapeutic. There was an attic above the kitchen which I set to work converting into a dining area with Dads help. It was a great success and we spent a lot of time up there. Poor Mum had an accident. She brought me a cup of coffee to the attic bedroom. She was prone to dizzy spells. She climbed the ladder; passed me the coffee; on her way down she lost her grip and tumbled to the floor. We had to get her to hospital by ambulance where they found she had a broken wrist. I was in the habit of going over to the bar once a week for a few drinks. On one occasion a local character sat beside me. He was a very large man. I had a few by then. He asked me who I was. I told him. He said he knew my father and his friend Bart Mathieson when they were young. He implied they were a couple of Nancy boys. I was drunk and by now my world was becoming some insane nightmare. I got in my car and drove out the single track road to the woods. I spent the night in the car there. The next day I lay on my bed in the attic looking at the ceiling totally numb. Everything I knew and believed in had been taken from me. If there was a God I asked him to take me now. My breathing became shallower and shallower. I had what can only be described as a revelation. I felt myself levitate from the bed towards the ceiling. There was a blinding flash of light and from that moment my path was clear. I knew what I had to do. I was going to return to San Francisco and start a new life. I was in no doubt about this.

NO
U
TURN

Chapter 21 San Francisco, again

1998 San Francisco again. I packed the car an old Chevy with my things and headed off on the familiar road to San Francisco. Art said I could stay at his till I sorted myself out. This was a good friend. We had not seen each other for years and had both had a wife or girlfriend along the way. I soon got a job. A good full time job; a company car; working for an up and coming housebuilder. My luck was changing. I was able to give Daisy my car and a substantial monthly payment for the children's welfare. My first job was at Mill Valley, California. The site was largely completed. It had lost its way in the final few homes. I was able to tidy things up and bring a bit of organisation to the table. That's what I do. It's not rocket science. On Wednesdays and weekends I tagged along to the pub with the lads. They had substantially not changed. They reminded me of the person I had once been. They didn't have to do anything. Just being amongst them was enough. The pub nearby which has changed its name several times since played Radiohead & Verve a lot. These were the Anthems to my recovery. Ray was playing squash at the time with Ian Brown. Ray & Bridget had 2 sons. The eldest won a bursary to University High School so they both went. Ian's children were there. That's how they met. They played at the squash courts there. I had never played squash but I tagged along. Ian was in similar circumstances to me. He was going through a difficult separation and divorce. It was becoming a theme of that era. Sisters were doing it for themselves. Ian had just taken possession of a large detached house in Russian Hill and was looking for sharers. I fitted the bill. I moved in there. Art likes his space which we all do. There was Ian, Shimmy (Ians partner), me, Cliff, Phil and various other extended family and friends along the way. The place had 3 storeys, big rooms, and a large back and front garden with off street parking, centrally located, perfect. It was a bit like a return to hippy days of the 70's as Shimmy was a character steeped in that era as we shall find out. I took the room at the top of the house. I can recommend house sharing for anyone getting over a marriage breakdown. Perhaps this one was a bit special. Every person that came through that house had an interesting story to tell. Ian like me was from a middle class background. He was the son of Gordon Brown and the nephew of Dan Brown, the writer. I could see a bit of Dan in his shambolic style of formal dress and thought processes to obscure realms. Shimmy was a child of the 60's older than Ian previously married with 3 daughters in their late teens. Her family had been blown apart from their idyllic lifestyle in the California countryside. Her husband unwisely started cultivating cannabis on an industrial scale. He was farm manager on an estate belonging to a prominent politician. He was now in jail. Ian met Shimmy when she was forced to move into Frisco. She rented a basement flat from a well-known actor. They met at the Nova Scotia on the Harbour where Shimmy was working behind the bar. Because of the circumstances Shimmy was a bit of a legend amongst the illegal substance, hippy fraternity of California and Frisco. Many appeared at our house at some point. Cliff was a friend of Ian's from school who was currently working as a tree surgeon. Phil was an extremely tall man from Manchester recently arrived in Frisco to make his fortune in IT. They would all meet up around 5 in the afternoons and share a pot of tea, a roll up or a joint, whatever you preferred in the large sitting room. A common theme in the house was nobody ever had any money. A lot of sharing and bartering went on. People had often arrived there during the day that had no money, no home, in transit between adventures. They all seemed to fit in as long as they didn't linger. Living at Chestnut Street brought an added dimension to my social life. I had my oldest friends the Lads I met when I came here 20 years ago, and now a new group I would meet through my new home. In time they all collided. We used to have regular Sunday dinners and irregular parties and garden gatherings. We never knew who was coming but all were welcome. Everything was shared. There was never enough. And always the same few who consumed more than they contributed. My children, Ian's children, Shimmy's children were regular visitors on visiting weekends and school holidays. We became regular visitors to Kennedys round the corner where John was the landlord. There were always lots of children at parties. I soon realised I was not the only person who had a marriage breakdown. I was just the first of many that I knew. By now Art was with Sara who worked at the industrial area where Art had worked for years as a forklift driver; logistics they call it now. She was divorced with two children and liked to join the gathering at Kennedys or the Horseshoe at the weekend. She moved in with Art and made some welcome changes to the place but it didn't last. Art likes his space and Sara and her kids were a handful. She moved to the other side of the Bay and remarried. I was in the need of some female company. I didn't feel ready for a relationship but I noticed that several bordellos had popped up around the neighbourhood. In my new world I had decided it was good for me to try everything once, don't comment if you haven't tried it. I went along and met Candy and was pleasantly surprised at the experience. I arranged to see her privately. We went on to have an arrangement where she came to Chestnut Street for fun in the evenings. She was a stunning blond like a favourite of mine at the time Cameron Diaz. I noticed from her arms she had problems. Once we went to the pub. When she had a few I could see she was a bit crazy. We played pool but I could see men were drawn to her. She was a trouble magnet. She wanted me to be her pimp. I thought, if I continued to see her I'd soon be in some kind of trouble. I stopped seeing her. However it got a monkey off my back. I saw her a while later with a nice little family. She looked settled.

Things went well at work. I worked at several sites in and around San Francisco, on what they liked to call their Flagship Projects. It made me feel good. I was called their Senior Site Manager. It was a good set up and I enjoyed it. As everything does it changed. They became more successful; rebranded; new Sales Director. The Sales Manager on my site was an Irish red head. She was friendly enough to begin with but turned against me. I heard the carpentry foreman and her colluded against me. These things made up my mind to move on. I seem to like to help a firm change from not much to something, but not to stay to be part of it. I heard that one of the co-directors had an affair with the sales director. It brought about the end of his marriage and split the firm. I was surprised to see them on TV later. They were living in garish splendour in a celebrity neighbourhood of the city. They had a garage for supercars that was better finished than a luxury home. They had designer yappy little dogs they doted on. Yuk! It all looked a bit sad in a rich way. When you are working full time on a building site time flies. You are so involved in the fast moving environment and the many things that require your attention to keep things moving at pace. It seems like you have blinked and a year has gone by. Socially you just have time for a relaxing drink, dinner, and a good night's sleep. At home, Al a mutual friend came to live with us in the little box room with his teenage girlfriend. Shimmy's teenage daughters stayed there from time to time. There was always a crisis in her family. Ian bore the brunt of the problems. Al liked to stir things up. Drama would often come to a head in the early evening when Ian came home late for dinner. He would be reprimanded at length, and reminded of all the difficulties Shimmy had to deal with. Al would make things worse by making jokes at Shimmy's expense. Occasionally Ian in exasperation would launch his dinner across the sitting room. Then go to his room for a lie down. Little domestic dramas such as this kept us amused. A typical weekend during this time was an evening at the pub with a table of a dozen or so friends. Saturdays was for relaxing and catching up with shopping and things I didn't get time for during the week. I was still running and would run a 10k circuit round the Dock of the Bay. Sunday we would have dinner in the late afternoon. There was the usual problem of who was contributing and who consuming. Often a few what I called liggers would turn up late and consume only. Once we were having pre dinner drinks at the pub and dinner was burnt damaging the kitchen. On another occasion Shimmy was gardening and had amassed a huge pile of dry cuttings in the heat of the summer which she lit. She came into the house screaming. The garden was on fire. I had to call the fire department to stop the resulting inferno spreading to the neighbours. On Shimmy's birthday many of her friends from the past appeared. They would gather in her bedroom bearing gifts of certain substances. She would not be seen the next day. The party would go on all night all over the house. The night club we rigged up in the basement was popular with the children. Phil purchased a sailing dingy. He was short of money so I bought a half share. We kept it down at the Bay. We spent many happy sunny days down there messing about on the water. All good things come to an end and eventually the landlord wanted his house back. I moved to a house share with a landlady in residence round the corner. My social life didn't take too much of a knock. Ian & Shimmy moved to Nob Hill so we didn't see so much of them. They were probably glad after all the teasing. Al moved to China Town and Phil and Kerry to a house in Pacific Heights.

Chapter 22 Millenium, Sophia

2000. I went to Chicago that Christmas. On my return I was introduced to a new housemate. Sophia had just arrived in Bristol at New Year from Catalonia and was working at the Marriot Hotel in hospitality, on reception. She made a good first impression on me. She had attractive Latin looks, stylish dress sense, and friendly manner. I took in on myself to be her local guide and soon we were an item much to the displeasure of the landlady. Sophia introduced me to a more civilised way of living that I was not accustomed to. I was not used to going into large hotels and restaurants. She taught me that I would always be welcomed in any luxury hotel. I had always thought I would be turned away if I was casually dressed. I went to places with Sophia I would not otherwise have done and enjoyed the experience. She met all my friends and was well liked. They too were introduced to fine dining. I also travelled to Spain and was introduced to her family. They were very civilised and welcomed me to their country as if I was family. I was 14 years older than Sonia but it didn't seem to matter. I was having fun. She was keen to see New York so I agreed to be her guide. We flew to New York. We spent a lovely weekend there in Spring time. Of course Sophia loved New York. She could not wait to move there. Up until then moving to New York had not been on my mind. However Sophia was changing my view on things. Work was not as appealing as it had been. The landlady was being difficult. We agreed to go together. Get a place together and have a go at New York life again. New York was booming again after many years of property misery. This would be good for me. I was at the peak of my powers as a Site Superintendent. I had good experience and I was the right age. We rented a garden flat in a nice big house in W88th Street on the Upper West Side. Phil gave us a lift up in his camper van. My company car had been returned. Sophia soon got a job in hospitality in the Hilton downtown. It took me longer to get a job. Eventually I did get a good job nearby as Site Superintendent on an exclusive little development. I could walk to work. We were happy enough for a long time and had trips to Chicago, California, and Spain. The children stayed with us during holidays. As we got to know each other Sophia told me she suffered from epilepsy. I was not a problem as I had a classmate at school who suffered. I knew how to deal with it. She had associated mental health issues that required medication. Sometimes her behaviour was beyond me. She could not have children. That was ok with me. I noticed she could have extremes of enthusiasm about places and jobs and then quickly change her mind. She wanted to go home and for me to come. We were going to get married but I had doubts. I didn't want to distance myself from my children, family and friends. She liked to maintain a higher standard of living than I was accustomed to. Her mum and dad came to stay with us in Manhattan at Christmas. I had to entertain them because Sophia was working till very late. It was often an issue that because I worked days and she worked till late we never spent time together. On this occasion it wasn't a problem. Her parents and I who weren't far off my age had a good Christmas Eve in a local restaurant. We went to a midnight carol service on our way home. We split for a while and she went to live in a flat share downtown. Probably a row brought about by our age difference or difficulties due to different ambitions. We stayed friends and I used to visit her. Sophia returned to Spain and resettled in a little town in the Pyrenees. She worked as an English language teacher. We kept in touch. I stayed with her in her flat for several weeks and we spoke about the possibility of me joining her there. I gave the idea a lot of thought. I was not comfortable. I didn't have the heart to tell her. I do not deal with difficult issues with people close to me the way I should. I don't discuss things. If there is no obvious answer, I come to a solution myself. I also knew that if we had a row it could lead to her fitting. I was increasingly uncomfortable for many reasons while I was there. Uppermost in my mind was that I would be too far from my children. I kept it to myself as best I could. We spent quite a bit of time with her Mum and Dad and it was becoming more and more obvious they wanted me to stay with her. By the time I got on the coach to go home I knew that was the last time we would be together. I waited till I knew she was in a safe environment with her parents till I let her know. I did not want to phone her in case she became emotional and unwell. I text her to say it was over. I know that is bad. I also knew with her health issues to do it face to face could be even more devastating. I did not want her to blame herself. I wanted her to blame me.

Chapter 23 Mystic

2003 Connecticut. I was at the apartment in Manhattan. Work was not coming in. I had given one months' notice to the landlord. Sophia was now living in Spain. I couldn't afford the rent. I had told the Agency I was leaving New York. My agent persisted in telling me to go for an interview with Try Homes in Connecticut. I went along and when they told me it was for a No 1 Site Manager on a new block of apartments. I was interested. It was a big job and I liked the people. I'd never been to or heard of Mystic which was a two and a half hour drive from the Upper West Side. By now I was driving a Pontiac Grand Prix. I had a shaky start at the site. Age and all the setbacks I had were starting to affect my confidence. The first few days it manifested itself in me losing my voice and sciatica. I covered up the back as best I could but my voice. By boss must have thought they made a mistake. I was staying in a B&B and at 1 point I could barely get out of bed with my back which I damaged moving stuff into storage. The landlady recommended a physiotherapist nearby. He was very good and he had me back in action quickly. I overcame my difficulties. Got my confidence back and started to get into the job. I moved into a little 1 bed flat in the heart of Mystic in Art School Yard. I found Mystic a bit suburban and dull after New York but it grew on me as I got to know it. It didn't take me long to settle in as I did not have much stuff. I liked the fact that my flat was at the top looking down on the shoppers going by. I was above a coffee shop and bakers so there were always nice aromas, if the window was open. Mystic has the best traditional market I have ever seen. The centre is a buzzing place and the suburbs are quiet. The harbour and park surroundings are beautiful. The job progressed well. It was a large 6 storey block of apartments with podium slab parking. It was traditional concrete and block construction with a tower crane. There were a large no of bricklayers and ground workers there but less than in recent times. As things progressed

I got an assistant Lee Summers who was quite a character. He had done a variety of jobs including films. Bit of a ladies man. After a while I was getting lonely and Lee encouraged me to go on internet dating. One photo caught my attention and after a little bit of correspondence I arranged to meet her for a drink. Rose wasn't quite what I was expecting from the photo. She admitted later it was an old photo. She was a character and I enjoyed her company. Rose was divorced. She had two teenage daughters and a large pointer dog. She lived in West Haven. She worked on payroll at New Haven Correctional Center. We started seeing each other. Rose knew the area better than me. She showed me round. She was probably the most popular girlfriend I had with friends and family. It was good. It added a dimension to my life that was missing. I was sharing a bit of family life. Watching her children grow up and have children of their own. Of course as time went by my demons would surface. I did not always enjoy the company of her extended family. She was my age. I preferred women younger than me. We came from different backgrounds. So there were doubts, which women instinctively latch on to. I'm sure Rose had doubts of her own. She had other admirers closer to home. So in time we went into a phase of splitting and getting back together again. My eldest Leyla was 17 by now and becoming too much of a handful for Daisy. It was arranged she would come to stay with me in Mystic. Shortly after she arrived I had booked to go to Spain and Leyla would have to look after herself till I returned. I didn't find out till I returned that she had gone to a night club. Her bag was lost or stolen including house keys. She had to spend the time I was away at the parent's home of a lad Paul she had met till I returned. Paul became Leyla's boyfriend and a big influence on her for several years. Leyla went on to work at the optician in town and train as an Optician including going to college. I went on to do several developments in Connecticut. Jim did well at school, particularly in Art and as a prefect. When he left school he was coming to stay with me in Mystic. Leyla was in a flat share nearby. I had to find a bigger place. I found a lovely place to rent in Willow Street. The house was in a lovely location with a nice back garden and a shed. It would be perfect for our needs. I moved in in the summer of 2006. Jim came down in time to start a course in Art at the local college. If he did well this would qualify him for entry to university the following year. He wanted to do a Degree in Fine Art. At Try Homes there had been changes in the set up that were not to my liking and I had left.

Chapter 24 Lily

I was making myself available for freelance roles and jobs around my neighbourhood. I immediately met my neighbours Jed and Amy who couldn't have been lovelier. Jed and Amy were very refined and actively interested in the Arts. During our time there Jim and I learnt a lot about art, theatre, music, local history; much of which was thanks to Jed and Amy. Jed was a former architect, lecturer, and artist and a radical political activist as a student. He was retired and now worked from a studio at the bottom of his garden. His work is often displayed at the Summer Exhibition in New York. I was impressed with his studio. I decided it would be a good idea to convert our shed into a studio for Jim. I set about it before he arrived and finished it off with his help. He was able to use it as his base for art and music. I bought him an electric guitar, a small amp, and an acoustic guitar. There was a lot of snow that Christmas. Christmas is a lovely and emotional time for families. My experience being divorced is that I accept that my children spend it with their Mum. My reason for this is that on a scale of 1-10 she would be more upset than me if they didn't spend it with her. I know some people would negotiate but I have never said otherwise. So I take what offers I can at Christmas and catch up with the children after. I have had some lovely Christmas at my brother Doug; with Sophia in Chicago & Spain; with Rose and family in West Haven. On this occasion it was just me at home in the snow. I decided to ignore Christmas. No decorations, dinner, tradition, church. I spent Christmas down in the studio teaching myself electric guitar. I hope Jed wasn't in his studio to hear me attempt to play Neil Young riffs and whine along. Jed and Amy were great entertainers and over the Christmas holiday they invited me for dinner. Another neighbour Kathy was invited. Kathy was my generation; a musician, she played flute with National Opera. She was a cheerful lass from Boston who was good company at dinner. Later on she returned the favour by inviting us to dinner. We had an enjoyable evening, the wine flowed. Just before we left she showed us her basement which she had just had converted into her studio. We were saying our goodbyes and I was following Jed and Amy up the basement stairs to get our coats. It was still a snow covered scene outside. Kathy held me back and told me to wait there while she saw them out. I was a bit surprised at her forthright approach. By now I had a few drinks and had no reason to complain. I spent the night there and more. Kathy was on tour with the opera. She asked me if I could renew her kitchen. That winter and spring I was working on her house and another nearby. She would do a performance then drive home; often from far away. I would be at her home by arrangement. This was quite a good arrangement for a while but familiarity breeds contempt. She was an independent, forthright girl and we clashed sometimes. In fact she really got on my nerves after not much time with her at all. I had noticed another woman who lived two doors up from me. I very rarely saw her. She used to arrive in a convertible Audi at odd times usually with family or a boyfriend. On one occasion I met her when I was returning from a run and she and her boyfriend were returning from a walk. I admired the way she looked in riding breeches and dark glasses. She had a loud voice and I could often hear her on her mobile early in the morning, I presumed in her garden. One sunny morning in Spring; Jim and I were doing some work out on the street. Sunny mornings always brought people out in the community for a chat. Lily opened her sash window wide and leaned out to talk to Annie next door. They were jokingly saying there was never a man around when needed. Lily was expecting visitors and her plasterer had not shown up to finish the painting of her lounge. I joined in the conversation. I realised I had an opportunity to get to know this women. I offered our services. Jim and I quickly painted the lounge in readiness for dinner that evening. It seemed there was a lot going on in that house; lots of phone calls and arrangements being made; always the offer of a cup of tea, or if it was after lunch, a beer, a glass of wine, or even champagne. Lily took an interest in Jim's art. She worked in the film industry which Jim was interested in. Lily was always disappearing off to meetings or lunch and wouldn't return till late if at all. I was intrigued. For a while I was a spectator. Saw her coming and going. Family and friends visiting; boyfriends; more than one; going off on trips abroad. There was always a lot of activity around Lily. People coming and going; flowers delivered; trips to the hairdresser. Everyone noticed when Lily arrived or left. For a while I was the friend two doors up. We shared a drink, a cup of tea, and I helped out around the house and garden. She had a party for family and friends. It started in the afternoon and went on till the following morning. All her family were there. Dad Adam, Mum Pam, Sister Julia, Brother in Law, their 3 children, neighbours, her boyfriend and friends from New York, ex-husband Charlie, staff from the pub at the Fighting Cocks. Kathy was there and put her arm around me like she owned me. I did not like that. Everyone noticed and made a point of reminding me. Old and young alike were playing tennis on xbox which was great fun. The party was great fun. It was a lovely sunny day. Half the guests went out to the garden. I was doing work in neighbour's homes at the time. Lily's boyfriend at the time, Malcolm turned up late with friends. They sat at the bottom of the garden being unsociable and left early. Lily got upset about this. I left in the afternoon but the party went on till the early hours and the staff from the pub stayed over; 1 lucky young man with Lily. He was a steady cam operator who Lily had known for a long time. There was always gossip in the street of Lily's bedroom activities. The neighbours were close enough to hear the occupants of the house next door. People kept their windows and doors open in good weather. As I got to know Lily she told me about her past. She grew up in suburbs of Manhattan. Her Dad, Adam now retired and living nearby in Mystic was a successful businessman. He had been in the business of fitting out hotels around the world. Her mum Pam helped as his p.a. and they had an office in Manhattan. Lily and her sister Julia went to a private school. They were well spoken and educated. Lily was very rebellious as a young teenager. She left home very young because she was upsetting her father. She was going clubbing and a big fan of punk band the Ramones. By 17 she was living in a bedsit in New York doing a variety of part time jobs. She met her husband Charlie through her punk lifestyle. Charlie was a punk with big Mohican hair. Soon after they met Charlie was badly beaten up by a jealous gang of Hells Angels. Lily knew one of them. She had rejected his advances in favour of Charlie. This was a terrifying ordeal for both of them. Lily had been a witness and as a result it drew them together. They moved to Mystic because they were too well known and an easy target in New York. In time they got married and established a business; supplying and maintaining camera equipment for the film industry, which was very busy. In time Lily also joined the business. They became so busy they never had children. Lily suffered from bipolar disorder. She was in a cycle of intense activity for a few months in the summer followed by seclusion and extreme depression in the winter. She did things to extremes. There was no balance. I began to spend time with her as a friend; having a drink; dinner; taking her nephews and niece out and about. Giving her and her parents bits of advice about building matters. I did fancy Lily but I was becoming aware of the complexity of her life and relationships. I didn't see a place for me. She also took Jim along to film sets and to see the business in New York. She let him use a very expensive film camera borrowed from the business. He loved all this. Lily had an old shed at the bottom of her garden. She said she would like to remove and replace it with a garden office/studio. She and Charlie had recently settled their divorce. Lily had received a large settlement. She had been working for the business when I met her. She was now planning to set up a complementary business to Charlie's business; an agency for steady cam operators to the film industry. She would work from the office at home. I set to work building Lily's Office. When you are a builder in someone's home you become part of the family in some respects. You become more aware of how they live on a daily basis. Lily's way of life was chaotic and dramatic. It was difficult to concentrate on anything you chose to do. You had to provide an audience for whatever drama was going on that day. A boyfriend that had upset or let her down; A man who was stalking her; A row with her parents or sister; An important meeting at lunchtime. So in between the many cups of tea; I started to clear the area and gather material for the office. After work I would usually have a drink with her before going home. From what I could see she had a boyfriend Malcolm she was unhappy with; another old boyfriend, a steady cam operator; she would have the odd fling with; a friend of her sisters who was stalking her; and a few others I knew who had their eye on her including me. Lily wasn't one for girlfriends. She preferred men. She was good at approaching men. She made them feel good about themselves. That did not last long. She was about to go on one of her regular jaunts. She was going to Costa Rica on this occasion. Her father Adam had recommended somewhere. There was a lot of intense activity in preparation. It was about the time of a festival in Mystic. The parade went up our street into the park. We had a note to tell us not to park in the street from 11am. I had made plans to deliver materials to Lily's that morning. This involved carrying the material through the house to the back garden. I got a bit delayed at the builder's yard. By the time I got to the street I only had 10 mins to offload the material. I did it as quick as I could. By now my neighbours who were stewards for the event were getting agitated. Lily had gone to Costa Rica so I locked up and went. I returned on Sunday afternoon. Adam was there. He was trying to get a big fat wood pigeon out of the lounge. I had left the back door open. Lily often did this. I should not have on this occasion. My relationship with Lily's parents was fine as long as I was the hired help. But they became suspicious of me if they thought I was anything more than that. I think it had something to do with being a Scot. It became like "Meet the Fockers." We referred to this incident later as "Pigeon Gate" in homage to "Watergate;" the Nixon political scandal. The look on Adams face was priceless. I helped him tidy up. In the next couple of days it became apparent that another crisis had developed concerning Lily. She had arrived in Costa Rica and decided the hotel was not up to her high standard. She was very upset. Phone calls were being made. Accommodation changed at great expense. Malc her boyfriend would fly out. Thankfully Pigeon Gate was forgotten about for now. I carried on with my work. When she returned a week later the family had been to the house making ready; fresh flowers; food in the fridge etc. Lily returned. The usual drama was relived; then family and friends went off. I continued with my work. During breaks for tea Lily opened up to me. She felt let down by her father who recommended the hotel. Her boyfriend had a nervous breakdown while he was there. Her steady cam boyfriend felt he couldn't cope with a relationship with Lily. Her sister's friend had come on too strong 1 evening and Lily had to tell him to leave forcibly. She would also talk to me about her plans for the new business. I was able to help with this having been a businessman of sorts, in the past. One evening we were watching a film together. I by now had strong feelings for Lily and told her so.

Thankfully it went ok and we became close from then on. It was not straight forward as you can imagine from what I have already written. I had come to the point that I wanted to take on Lily as my partner knowing about her past and wanting to help to make the future better. As I write this I can see the pitfalls. Is it wise to enter into a relationship in order to make someone's life better? Now I can look at and understand my mistakes and failings. In the charged atmosphere of love, I cannot, obviously. The next month was great. We were in love. Basically we shut the door to the world and spent it in each other's company. The word must have gone round that I was more than the hired help and everyone left us alone. In time this would change but it was great while it lasted. At this time I did not realise the extent of Lily's illness and for how long it had affected her, her friends, and family. And also what affect it would have on me. For a long time my feelings for Lily were so strong I was prepared to make many sacrifices to be with her. I was devoted to her. She brought a lot to my life that was missing without her. Eventually we had to come out of the bubble and "Meet the Fockers". Adam & Pam took it very badly. For a long time, they would not come to the house, or have anything to do with me. It was pretty much the same for her sister's family. Boyfriends kept their distance but continued to text, phone, send flowers and gifts which was annoying. Ex-husband Charlie remained friends and I liked him. I helped him with a building problem he had on a house he was renovating in New York. I was slightly put out, being alienated by family. Being a Scot in USA, I was used to it. In some ways it was a blessing. Familiarity breeds contempt. Keep your enemies close. As an unknown quantity they were wary. Later when they got to know I was just another human being it would be different. We had a lovely summer. The weather was lovely. The office was completed. Lily established her agency. We went on trips to the countryside in Lily's new Saab convertible. On my birthday Lily treated me to a long weekend in a luxury suite in a 5 star hotel in Costa Rica. When I went on the terrace there was an ocean liner with a Scottish flag in front of me. I joked she arranged that too. It was during this trip I became uneasy. My demons surfaced. Lily had told me she had been here before in this hotel. For a hen night I believe. She told me they had gone to a club on the beach where they had a wild time. The other girls had one night stands. She wanted to go to the same place again. I had not liked what she had told me but I agreed to go. Lily was dressed in a tiny top, high cut jean shorts and a straw cowboy hat she just bought. She looked good; but could be mistaken for a hooker. I went along but was in a mood. I didn't enter into the spirit. It was probably the first time Lily had seen me in one of my moods. I tried to make light of it. I came round eventually but this was a warning. It was a reminder to me that there was a side to me that I could not control; that was not good for any relationship. The flowers, gifts, texts continued to arrive for Lily. I ignored them but they annoyed me. I never said anything. Summer went and winter came. Lily's health declined with the weather. Her appetite and enthusiasm dwindled. She was less concerned about her appearance. She went out less. She was drinking, smoking a lot, and on medication. I did what I could. I made sure we had dinner in the evenings and made her wellbeing my priority. Not work. If I was out all day at work she went into more of a decline. My children became her extended family. I think it was good for her to have that. I know it annoyed Daisy that she liked and encouraged them with their careers. It also took her out of herself preparing family meals. Agency work came in from time to time. I would go off to New York on an assignment for 2 or 3 months. When I did this I could see her decline. I was grateful when the assignment ended so I could spend more time with her. I was concerned about this. It was not good for business to be caring. I also worried she was going on assignments of her own when I was not around that were unfaithful to me. I went to greater lengths with Lily than I would have for anyone else not to react. Simply because I was devoted to her and I wanted her. When she was not well I tried to make her better. In time I would find out from doctors I was wasting my time. I was told Lily had to want to be better and make herself better. She would turn against me for trying. We shared a lot of wonderful times together. I just felt happy being with her and when I was driving back from New York I looked forward to seeing her. Our life together in Mystic became a soap opera. Lily is such a big character there were many people who had a piece of her. I was punching above my weight. A lot of gossip went on. Difficulties arose in our life through other people's expectations. Lily could be unwise, mischievous, and naïve about the company she kept. I could never work out which. I knew there were many that wanted to harm us; to break us up. Not many were happy for us. As I write this I think. Is this my fault? Is this my problem? Does this become jealousy? I kept any concerns that I had to myself but it came to a head. Lily decided to go into NewYork to meet Malc and friends. She didn't return that evening and said she was staying over at some friends. I went to work in New York the following day and returned the following evening. Lily arrived all glammed up. When I had last seen her she had not been. We shared a bottle of champagne. I asked for an explanation and her response was not convincing. I pressed her. She spat out in my face, yes I was with Malcolm and yes I spent the night with him. I jabbed her on the mouth, more for affect, than to hurt, in the spur of the moment. I immediately realised what I had done, to my horror. Lily was by now very agitated and rushing about the house. I was shocked that it had come to this and left immediately.

Chapter 24 Lily

I got in the Pontiac and drove. I had nowhere to go. I lived with Lily. I no longer rented my house. Jim had moved to college in San Francisco. I drove around for a bit and then decided to drive to the site in New York. The security guard was surprised to see me. I was on good terms with him and explained what had happened. I spent the night in the car. The next evening I moved into B&B in Mystic. Lily went back to Malc. I moved into a rented apartment on the other side of Mystic. I felt very empty for a long time and blamed myself. I was lonely and eventually I got in touch with Rose again. We tried to go back where we left off but it didn't feel the same. Trust had gone. Rose had moved on. I was different. I still loved Lily. Out of the blue sometime later Lily phoned me. I was at Roses home. Lily told me she had recently attempted suicide but she was alright now. She was letting me know in case I heard through the grapevine. I was shocked. Rose could tell something was wrong so I told her. I arranged to meet Lily in a pub in Mystic. She was looking good. She told me she had gone back to Malc. He had made a big fuss of her. He was rich apparently. Exotic holidays, dinners, lots of presents. Promises of marriage and a new life in the country: a dream come true for her family and friends. But, on holiday recently he had taken to his bed with extreme depression and said he couldn't do it. Well I tried not to show my glee and mumbled something to the effect I was sorry. I always thought he was gay. No disrespect intended. We had a few drinks. Lily said she had cooked. Too much for one; would I like to something to eat. We went back to hers which felt strange. We had dinner. My favourite Spaghetti Bolognese. We listened to music. Lily told me the details of her attempted suicide. It sounded like a call for help but serious nevertheless. She had been at home. Robin, one of her suitors had been round to try to make things right when she was upset. She had sent him away. She got more upset, drunk too much, took too much medication. She phoned Charlie in a state. He got medical assistance. I stayed the night and got up early to collect my things and go to work the next day. We got back together again. I moved back into Lily's. By now her family had formed a very low opinion of me and they stayed away for a long time. There was still a few of Lily's men friends including Malc staying in contact which was annoying. I put them to the back of my mind and convinced myself they were gay. Before they had split Malc had put Lily onto an opportunity for a fabulous job as PA to a CEO of a company that invested in gold mining. Her agency never really got off the ground. The job was in Manhattan. Lily got the job and started commuting into Manhattan with me. I was working in Hell's Kitchen at the time but would soon move to a hotel renovation near City Hall. So for a while we became busy commuters. Family and friends had stepped into the background a bit but not completely. Lily's neighbour was a problem. She was a sad lonely woman who we had both been friendly with and assisted in the past. She had turned against both of us and behaved badly towards us since. We would get up early. Travel to New York. Meet after work. Have a drink, maybe something to eat and travel back. Lily had done this for many years when she was married and it helped her. She also continued to do a few shifts down at the Fighting Cocks. She got my son Jim a job there and he went on to work in bars after that. When the Agency was quiet she started working down there. She was almost managing the place as the manager spent little time there. There was also a group of men there with too much time on their hands. I knew they had their eye on Lily. I was not only visiting the bar for pleasure but setting down a marker that I was there. They weren't sure how far they could go with a brooding Scot lurking nearby. We had a little group that did quiz night. I used to walk down at close for a quick drink and to walk home with Lily when she had cashed up. By now it was becoming clear to me that Lily not just liked a drink. She was a full blown alcoholic. Her lifestyle was based around her consumption of alcohol which started at noon and finished when she fell asleep. She didn't appear to suffer from hangovers like mere mortals, myself included. I began to take the view that I was enabling her in some way. Although she was quite happy to walk into any bar on her own and become the life and soul of the place. I had seen a woman in bars in Mystic when I first arrived who was similar to Lily but 10 years older. I had watched her deteriorate over the years. I did not want this to happen to Lily. Now that I was aware I started to reduce my consumption hoping that it would have an effect on her. I enjoyed a drink but I couldn't keep up with Lily. I think my drinking with her made it ok in some way. Lily worked as a PA. Lily worked for Charlie's firm in Film & Media. Her role was many and varied. Charlie, bless him knowing that Lily had health issues to deal with from time to time allowed her a degree of flexibility. I had let Lily be my PA on occasions when I needed assistance. Lily will enter into things with a full heart. Working for Charlie she was used to a degree of freedom and flexibility in how she worked. This is not always what is required. She was hired as PA for a CEO of a Company in Gold Mining. He was a pillar of the establishment who travelled a lot. He needed a PA who would sort out the details of his busy life every day. Apparently that did not happen. Lily possibly strayed from her remit. Maybe that's unfair. I'm sure she made a reasonable contribution. I suspect the media business worked differently. I see Lily as a highly creative, intelligent, influential person. I don't see her as a 9-5 work horse for an institution. After a six month trial she was released. Increasingly she was feeling the pressure of the demands of the job. Increasingly she smelt of alcohol. She was pickled. It was oozing from her pours. If I could smell it, I'm sure they could. The day she was released she phoned me. It was a big shock and she was very upset. I met her in City Hall Park. I helped her pick up a few things from the office. We went and sat on a bench at Rockefeller Park and she cried. We made our way back to the car. On the way we passed the Smyth Hotel and I treated her to afternoon tea to help cheer her up. By the time we got back to Mystic she was feeling a lot better. Things settled down a bit. Winter was coming so Lily was spending more time at home. She was worried she would lose the house. There were bags full of bills and letters from debt collectors she had not opened in the office. I declared myself bankrupt in 2009. This was the consequences of a career in construction, divorce, and three children. There was never enough to go round. We had been to San Francisco a couple of times and Lily liked it there. She needed to get away. Our circumstances at the time led to us talking about selling up and moving on. Lily could get a good price for her house at the time. Recent events had made her feel she wanted space from family and friends. It would stop the worry of the bailiffs appearing at the door. She could pay off debts. This decision was driven by Lily. Not me. I was getting fed up with her family and friend's too. From my perspective it appealed to the gypsy in me. I felt I had spent a wonderful time in Mystic and New York but it was time to move on. I was getting to an age I was not the generation for New York and I was tiring of Mystic. So the house went on the market and was sold quite quickly. It took ages to pack up and move. Lily had so much stuff. She also had storage. Everything had to be gone through. Decisions had to be made about what to do with it. Everything was a memory that had to be relived. A lot went to the dump. A lot went into storage. A lot was re distributed to family and friends. It was a very emotional business.

Chapter 25 San Francisco with Lily

When the house was sold we drove to San Francisco in our 2 VWs Swampy & Bertie as Lily called them. It was a 5 day drive stopping in motels. It was a journey we both needed. Initially we stayed in one of our favourite places the Radisson Blu in a Duplex suite on the 16th floor overlooking the Bay. I was determined to make Lily's introduction to San Francisco a pleasant one. Remembering what my own had been 30 years previously. We started looking for somewhere more permanent to live. I knew Frisco better than Lily and I soon found a place I thought was suitable. It was a modern townhouse on Sea Cliff Avenue with a view of the Golden Gate. It was expensive to rent for San Francisco but good value by New York standards. We moved in and had a furniture van bring stuff from storage and bought some new stuff. Once it was sorted out we had a lovely place to live with plenty room for visiting friends and family. I had been making efforts to resolve any differences with Lily's family. Work was the next thing to be resolved. I found it difficult to begin with because I was the new kid on the block again and in some respects despite a good CV and good experience you have to start again. I felt I had a duty to entertain Lily as she was new to the city so I made sure we had plenty outings to show her round. But to be fair we had the best spot in town right where we lived. We had a 1st floor sitting room with a balcony overlooking the bay where there was always plenty of activity on and off the water to keep our interest. This was the very spot where Phil and I sailed the dingy all these years ago. Jim was in town studying for his Fine Arts degree at the Academy of Art and I think he was surprised to find I was well established in Frisco. Had he forgotten his childhood days here? Lily was lucky with her job hunting. We were walking up Grant Avenue one day when she noticed a green coat in a tailor's window she liked the look of. I said I would buy it for her as I thought it suited her. We went in and had a look round, bought the coat. Lily likes to talk and struck up a conversation with the Manager Emily who was very cheerful and friendly. Lily said she was new in town and looking for a temp job. Emily said she was trying to fill a position at the moment and gave Lily an application. Of course she got the job and went on to be a key member of staff. Lily would do 2 or 3 days a week at Larry's which she enjoyed. Frankly I think this was the right balance of work for her. She was home sick and spent a lot of time on the phone to her mum and made arrangements to travel home for long weekends. This was a bit ironic as she had wanted to get away. I wasn't feeling good at that time as I was finding it hard to get a job. I introduced Lily to my friends Art, Jet, Ray, Beth which was fine but there were a couple of incidents I regret. Given what had happened in the past I did not fully trust Lily. In fact, knowing myself now, I don't really trust anyone. That's a bit of a sad revelation but the sum total of my life experience has brought me to this point. I decided to keep a bit of distance from my mates because I felt Lily was too friendly with Jet in particular. I probably came to this conclusion at a time when my self-esteem was low. I was back in San Francisco amongst my mates and new girlfriend. Everyone was working and I was not. At Hogmanay we met in the Merchants round the corner where John was now the landlord. I had started drinking in the afternoon and got a bit morose. In the evening and went home without Lily. Bad behaviour I know. I have some bad stuff in me that I don't understand and can't control. I had another concern that I hadn't spoken to Lily about. Lily had 2 mobile phones. I could hear it sounding regularly as texts came in. She never commented. At one low point I resolved to throw the phone in the Bay. I got the opportunity one evening when she had fallen asleep and left her phone in the sitting room. And that's what I did. It didn't make any difference she bought another one. Flowers and presents continued to arrive at the house from time to time from Malc. This was annoying. I often thought about going to his place of work which was next door to Charlie's place and having it out with him. When I thought about it I thought it was a dangerous strategy that would probably backfire on me. Anyway I hadn't had a fight since I was a schoolboy. I didn't want to comment on any of this to Lily because I didn't want a row. In my experience it usually comes back to it's my problem. She was going home regularly and extending her stay once she was there. Although this was a concern most of the time we were good together. I was devoted to Lily. I propped her up during the bad times and loved to see her blossom in the good times. Lily's addiction was getting worse. We had spoken about her getting treatment in the past but it never happened. There was always a reason not to. I spoke to our doctor on more than 1 occasion but because of patient confidentiality he was limited what he could say. He did however try to help by prescribing medication to put Lily off alcohol and cigarettes but it only had a limited effect. He did say to me that in San Francisco he dealt with many people with addiction problems. In his experience 99% of them never get better. This came as a bit of a shock. But I could understand what he said from my experience of Lily trying and failing to get better. We invited Lily's family to stay with us and these visits went well and I started to go with Lily to Mystic to see them. After a long period of me having no work or short assignments I got a job at Skanska on primary schools which was the only good opportunity I had since I came to San Francisco. They had a more professional way of doing things than most. Their managers came from their graduate recruitment programme and so were of a higher calibre than is the norm in construction. They also used IT and BIM more than most. I enjoyed this environment. After a year and a half's tenancy at Sea Cliff Avenue our landlords were looking to move back. We had to find somewhere new to stay. We looked at many places but Lily was not happy with any of them. I would find out later she had an agenda that I was not aware of. In the end when we were close to having to move out with nowhere to stay I found a 2 bed flat nearby which was sufficient for our needs. Lily was not in approval but I insisted it was our only option. Our last place had been an indulgence. This was a practical option we could afford. I also thought that if Lily left me I could afford the rent alone. Lily was going through a bad patch. Initially I had to drag her along with me but I was convinced this place would be ok for us. It wasn't about being nice for entertaining her family. I went to a lot of effort with the layout to get it so she would like it. In time I think she did. There were several things that happened during this time that changed me from my total devotion to Lily to self-preservation. Her father took ill. It became terminal cancer. Lily had a difficult relationship with her father. There was love there but a lot of conflict. He was a traditional right wing kind of guy. She was a radical left winger. He found her illness difficult to address and ignored it. She was going through a difficult time in herself and this was making it worse. She would spend long periods deep in thought or listening to music. Not caring about her appearance. Sitting on the balcony smoking and drinking. However when work called she was able to pull herself together and present a totally different image which I found remarkable. I was by now attending meetings of Al Anon at a local church hall. Al Anon is a group meeting for the friends and family of people with addiction problems. I only went to one meeting. There was 8-10 people sat in a circle in the church hall. One by one we had to tell the group why we were there. I was struck by the fact that although each person had different circumstances the story was the same. They all had someone close to them with addiction problems. They all wanted to help them get better. The more they tried to help the more their loved one turned against them. Nothing got better and they felt lost and upset. The counsellor summarised that this was always the way. The addict had to want to change. They have no conscience. You have to think of yourself. If you don't, you will be damaged. This was a revelation and a relief for me. I had been trying to do all kinds of things to make things better for years. I was suffering terribly inside and had no one to share my pain with. However I was determined to learn from what I had heard. I wanted to save myself. I didn't feel I had to go back to another meeting. I had seen the writing on the wall. I concentrated with my work. I continued to give Lily all my love and support. A little part of my head was now ruling my heart. During this time Lily did some things that I could not condone. At her work she decided in collaboration with a colleague Seb from Venezuela to turn against her boss Emily. Together they had made a list of things that in their opinion Emily had done incorrectly. Lily scheduled a meeting with the Area Manager to talk about their concerns. I strongly disagreed with what she was doing. She was being a grass as far as I was concerned. I was also concerned with the influence of Seb who was gay. She was taking an interest in all things gay and going to gay pride. No disrespect, but she was not gay. She was meeting Seb for a drink at the Beer Barge near where we lived and I innocently said I would come along. I sat at a table with them. I knew Seb. He had fitted me for my suit which I wore at Jacks graduation. I was giving him the evil eye. I told him what I thought of their plans. I made it clear what I thought of him. Lily and he stormed out and left me to finish my drink. I was pleased to have my say. She left me for a while. I can't remember where or what she did. She had the meeting and no good came of it. Emily who was on maternity leave was suspended. Lily lost her job. On another occasion we went to the Beer Barge for a drink in the early evening. We would often sit on a narrow walkway on the side where Lily could have a smoke. On this occasion she produced the aforementioned phone from her bag which was wrapped in a ribbon with some letters and a photo. She was going to throw them in the harbour. Ironic I thought. She volunteered to show me the contents first. The scan photo was apparently a photo of her unborn child with Malc which she lost. This was the first I had heard of this. I was always been reasonably sure she could not have children. Otherwise she would surely have done so when she was with Charlie. She knew from early on I had a vasectomy after Jack was born. Three children was plenty for me and the world. I couldn't see anything I could distinguish as a child, from the photo. The rest was love letters apparently. Any way she had decided she wanted to put all that behind her, for reasons she didn't say, and threw the bundle in the water. Well long overdue I thought. Alan was terminally ill in hospital. We travelled to Mystic to visit. Our relationship had healed by now and I held his hand as I spoke to him in bed in hospital. When he died Lily had been spending more time with her mum in Mystic. It was a sad but lovely occasion. Many people were there that I knew. It was a solemn occasion. I was there to support Lily. When she came back to San Francisco she was in a bad way for a long time. She was grieving but it was more so because of her condition. She would stay up late into the night playing music and crying. I was working for Skanska at the time and having to get up early. Eventually I had to tell her to tone it down a bit because I couldn't sleep. In time she started to recover from grief. She traded in Bertie the VW for a cheaper convertible Renault. I didn't think it was a good move. She had done it without saying anything to me. I thought this was odd. I think she still had debts hanging over her that I didn't know about. She was worrying that her savings were dwindling. We had rows about that. She blamed me. I worked out how much drinking and smoking cost over the five years I had known her. It was a shocking amount. She chose to ignore that. We had been together on and off for five years. I was reviewing the situation. I was thinking we either get married or go our separate ways. If I was using my head I would say without hesitation that we split but I loved Lily. There had never been a practical reason for us to stay together. But we did. She took off in her car one day. Did not say where she was going. I got in contact and she said she was down the California coast looking at art. Recently she had mentioned an artist she was interested in. I thought I would Google the artist. Thinking I bet he's good looking. I knew her. Of course he was. His art was not to my taste. She came home and told me she had taken off to clear her head. She had gone to the artist's studio and he had shown her round. She bought some art. They sat on the beach sharing a glass of wine. I could tell from her tone she had not been received as openly as she imagined. Perhaps he had a wife or a girlfriend. I was relieved.

On another occasion I had to take off at short notice. Leyla had taken ill. It was an emergency. I borrowed Lily's car; travelled to Mystic. Met Bekka, stayed at her flat in Mystic. Picked up Leyla's things and tidied her flat; picked up Leyla from Pauls parent's house; drove her home to Daisy's home in Rockport; then travelled back to San Francisco.

One evening we were at home after dinner. Lily by now was quite drunk. My daughter Leyla phoned. It's fair to say that Lily spent a lot more time on the phone than me. Leyla had recently been ill. I hadn't spoken to her since I had taken her to Daisy's. I was anxious to know how she was. As I was speaking I could see out of the corner of my eye that Lily was irritated that I was on the phone to Leyla. I was getting annoyed because she wouldn't give me space to make this call. She came and sat beside me and was making faces, raising her eyebrows as Leyla spoke. Lily could hear what she was saying. Leyla said something that made Lily raise her middle finger in response. I grabbed her hard by the wrist and pushed her finger back into her nose hard. She stormed into the bedroom. I told Leyla what happened and finished the call. I sat in the lounge for a long time; terribly upset. I was thinking about the past; everything that had happened between Lily and I; the fact that I had lost my temper for the second time. I came to a decision. It would not happen again. Lily eventually came back into the room. I told her we cannot be together anymore. It's over. Lily wanted me to move out. After some thought I said. No I am not moving out. I found this place. I like this place. I'm staying here. You are moving out. She was absolutely furious and left the room slamming the door off its hinges.

PART 3 MENSCH

Chapter 26 Scotland

My memory of what happened after that is a bit blurred. I think I was working at a school extension nearby at the time. This was a good job and I had a good crowd around me. It was summer 2012. I was 55 years old. I resolved never to have another close relationship. It was too dangerous for me. I immersed myself in the job which ran till the children went back to school in September. I had given my notice to quit the flat. I had some business to attend to in Scotland. I flew to Prestwick in Scotland. Aunt Mays bungalow in Penninghame, Wigtownshire had been on the market since she died in 2007. It had not sold and the price was dropping. Lily had not been in touch but I suspected she wasn't far away. I told her what I was doing and gave her first option on the flat. She took it. So when the kids went back to School there wasn't an assignment for me. I put what I didn't need in storage and returned to Scotland. The work on primary schools was seasonal and the boss said he would let me know if he needed me. I stayed at Judy's place at the Station guest house till I got the bungalow in a condition to stay in. It had been empty for a while. May had been in a care home with dementia. The house had not been cared for by the last tenants. I spent the first week getting a bedroom, sitting room, bathroom, kitchen ready for me including buying a new bed and starting decorating. I was able to move in after a week. I had a skip for all the rubbish. There was a lot old furniture, carpets and curtains and rubbish. Some previous tenants had painted walls dark colours, pink, purple, brown that wasn't doing anything for the place. I figured a good airing and a fresh coat of paint would do a lot. The garden didn't look very appealing. Some tenants had built a fenced area at the back to keep a dog in. That had to go. There had been a gardener keeping the garden but I wasn't impressed with their input so I instructed the estate agents to tell them they were not required. There was a large area of jungle before you could get to the boundary at the bottom of the garden. I would clear this. From time to time passers-by would ask me what I was doing. I would tell them I was doing up the house to sell or maybe I would buy it myself. I figured that by saying that if anyone was interested it might prompt them to make a move. The price was ridiculously low at less than £100,000 for a detached 3 bed bungalow with a big garden. When the house was sold the family solicitors had been instructed to split the proceeds between her nephews and nieces. Myself, John, Doug, Jean my brothers and sister and Ailsa, Jes, Robin, Brad my cousins on the South Coast. As things progressed I thought about buying it. I didn't feel inclined to take out a mortgage. Bearing in mind I was recently bankrupt. I had to find John once more. My brother had a tenancy of a pub in Chicago and absconded to Europe when he was a young man. He was difficult to locate but I need to find him to tell him he was a beneficiary of Mays will. I had a stroke of luck with that. Leyla found him via Facebook. He was living in the Western Isles. A friend of Leyla's knew him. He was working in a restaurant there. I was able to contact him and pass his address to solicitors. He came to Wigtownshire to settle things. I asked the family if anyone was interested in keeping the place in the family. There was no interest. John phoned me one evening drunk and told me he had no interest and I should have no interest as Penninghame was a "backwater". I was annoyed at him saying that. I was annoyed he phoned me drunk after all these years. I was annoyed he had not been at Mums funeral and had not been there to see her deterioration largely due to his disappearance. I gave him a piece of my mind and told him not to phone me unless he was sober. What I meant was never contact me again. I never will. Settling in was difficult. The pace of life was completely different to what I was used to. I had to remind myself to concentrate on getting the house sold. I also want to climb hills and get to know the land as my Grandfather had. The sense of the day is long and no instant entertainment. Make of it what you will. Embrace it and make good use of it. For if you do not it will surely destroy you. I have been out. I have seen other lives. I have seen other places. And I have enjoyed it. But now I am in the last phase of my life. This is my choice. The loneliness is a small price to pay for viewing the world from this place. And I have a feeling that here there is more for me to look forward to than I can imagine. I have a hint of that from my grandfather's writing. Most of which was done in the final phase of his life. There is Japanese philosophy that says life is divided in three. I continued working on the house. A few people came to view. I stayed there till Spring. During my time there I started getting out in the Galloway Hills. It was a bit hit and miss to begin with. I had maps and a compass, Grandfathers books. But I found there was a lot to learn. There are obvious routes like the path from Bruce's Stone to the top of the Merrick. The Southern Upland Way; Loch Valley; past Cumloden up to Auchinleck and the forest roads beyond; The Old Edinburgh Road; The Big Country Route; and many more. I would set out without previous knowledge of routes. Without much idea of how long it takes to cover say seven miles in the hills. Often the hardest part is the beginning and the end; the difficulty of finding a route onto the higher ground; close to farm steading; fields with beasts. Often the lower ground in Galloway is difficult to cross without paths and many hazards; tussocks, holes, unseen burns beneath the surface, bogs. The lead in's and out of your destination can be long and tiring if you are inexperienced. In time you develop a familiarity with the Galloway Hills that enables you to have the right things with you. Not too much stuff. OS Locate on your mobile phone is very useful; always a close eye on the weather forecast. Pick your moments. Pick your routes carefully. A full day on the hills can be exhausting. I have learnt to use my mountain bike and the old Pug I bought for forest roads to reccy routes and access before I approach hill tops. The whole process of getting to know the Galloway Hills is like a huge jigsaw puzzle. I find it very interesting and exhilarating. Along the way you get a tremendous sense of history. Sometimes you feel you have returned to the times of the Jacobite Rebellions, the Covenanters, or the Levellers, when walking in moody isolated places. There is a certain fear of this exploration on your own but there is also a reward. The reward is the successful challenge of what you set out to do; the beauty of the scenery and nature all around you. The ability to do the physical challenge; the challenge of map reading and location; the rare knowledge that there is something spiritually fulfilling; being alone in a place that was home long ago. Long before towns and roads and the human race was established in places of security, together. We were removed from the land and put in towns by the landowners of the time. The monarchy took the land away from the people and gave it to managers they trusted and honoured.

Chapter 26 San Francisco, Full Circle

In the **Spring of 2013** I got a phone call from Geoff Talor at Skanska while I was out walking to say there was an assignment at a primary school in San Francisco. Was I interested? Yes I was. Aunt May's house was sold. Mission accomplished. I was coming round to the way of thinking that I would return to Galloway to retire. With Mays passing there was no family left here. Maybe I should fly the McClain flag. I would take whatever opportunities I got in between times. I put all my stuff in storage and set off to San Francisco. I had arranged to stay at Arts till I got somewhere to stay. It was a "bitter sweet symphony" once again returning to Frisco but I soon involved myself in the familiar work of primary schools. I had a text from Lily to say she had relocated happily to rural California. I do not know the details but I am grateful to know she still lives. I soon got a room in a house in nearby Larkin Street with a live in landlady Lily ironically. It was a nice room with a view over the rooftops to the Suspension bridge and the Bay where I could watch the sun go down in the evening and balloons take off and float over the city. I was working at a new Primary School in North Beach so I was able to walk to work. Jim was still in town living with Juliet and working at the Beer Barge. I could barely bring myself to cross to that side of the Bay while I lived at Larkin Street. I would meet the lads at the Orchard House and the Hare mainly. During this time I kept in practice with my hillwalking by walking in the Marin headlands, Bernal Heights, Angel Island, Presidio, Muir Woods. And the High Sierra Music festival in Quincy CA. I spent a year at Larkin Street. The landlady sold the house and moved to be closer to her daughter in Manchester. I moved to a new bedsit in Francisco Street which was difficult to find. Rentals in Frisco were becoming expensive as the city's popularity as a place to live continued to grow**. May 2014.** This was a nice house with the landlady Edi in residence and her partner working in New York during the week where he had his own place. The room was too small but I was desperate. During my time at Francisco Street I got to know Edi, Dave her partner, James the West Highland terrier, Annie across the road and her family, David who had the room next door to me. Bene, who lodged at Annie's. We had what we called Lodger night where we gathered together and had something to eat and drink. It was fun. I had back trouble while I was there; recurrence of an old problem. I think the bed was too soft. I went to a physio at the tennis club. That didn't help much. I then found a Thai massage practitioner. That combined with walking and swimming helped a lot. To begin with I worked at Oasis Academy in North Beach but I was soon moved to Fairlawn Primary School in Lafayette Park. A magnificent building built in the 1890s where Cary Grant went to school before he went to Hollywood to be a film star. By now I felt I had come full circle in San Francisco I was living and working in the area I started in 40 years previously. The firm I started for GJ Construction was now called Kitto which was the name of the Group when I started. They were renovating and renewing all the doors and windows on the job. I was on this job till December 2015. This was a problem job to begin with. The 2 managers on the job were old school. They did not have the modern skills you need for this job. It soon became obvious to me they were out of their depth. During my time at Skanska I had now done several jobs. The boss Geoff Talor put me on jobs he was concerned about. By now everybody knew that and they were not pleased to see me. To begin with I couldn't do much even though I knew there was a lot wrong. The 2 guys in charge were all talk. They liked to be one of the boys on site. You have to keep authority. They had a bad influence on the men. You see this a lot in the industry. You have to be strong to get rid of these sorts. Events conspired to change things. There was an accident. One of the roofers fell through the roof and was quite seriously injured. I was First Aider on the scene. The following day the manager was larking about with the scaffolders and injured himself shadow-boxing. He stubbed his toe on a metal ladder lying on the ground. There was an enquiry involving HSE. Eventually after a lot of nonsense being reported by his assistant the truth came out. He was suspended. More supervision and changes in practices was asked for. My old boss from Oasis was called in as Project Manager. By now I had taken on many of the structural openings that the old manager had struggled with. He had been there for a year and hardly completed any of the 40 or 50 required. This was limiting progress. Unfortunately his assistant was still there. He actively tried to turn the men against me by talking to them about me behind my back. I had reprimanded him for parking his car in a place that was blocking us doing some work on a Saturday morning. He went home in the huff halfway through a shift. I don't think he spoke to me after that till he left thankfully. I was getting my head round the structural stuff. John eventually arrived. Realising the importance of the temporary works he got involved. Eventually he caught up with what I was doing. I n September 2015 many of the other school jobs in the city handed over. Skanska needed to place all their employees and reduce their freelancers of which I was one. I escaped being laid off initially. By December it was obvious there were too many managers. Geoff supplemented inexperienced payroll staff with older experienced hands like myself. This was unpopular in some quarters close to me. I could see it coming and new my time had come. It still hurt. I gave notice at the house which was long overdue and got myself organised to move again; but where to? I had been moving in ever decreasing circles all my adult life like a gypsy. I never had anywhere I called home. Maybe I should give the clan homeland a try. We had no family presence there since Aunt May passed.

Chapter 28 Western Isles

Jan 2016 Penninghame, Wigtownshire. I returned to Penninghame with a car completely full of my things and booked into Judy's place at the Station Guest House. I had a look at several places and quickly decided to take the house I am in because it ticked a lot of boxes. I had booked flights and accommodation in Nice over New Year. I decided to move into the house on my return. I went up to spend time with family and friends in Fife at Christmas and flew to Nice from Liverpool the day after Boxing Day. I had to drive to Liverpool in the VW. I had a lovely time in Nice relaxing in an apartment just off the promenade. I would promenade up and down every morning in between meals as one does there. I noticed on Sky news while I was there that Penninghame was making the news headlines. This was a rare event. The Cree had burst its banks. The town was flooding. It was strange to see people that I recognised being interviewed amongst the devastating flood. On my return the guest house was full of people who had been made homeless. One old gentleman Nicky who was well known in the town on his mobility scooter was having difficulties. He lived in the ground floor of the Mill in Minnigaff which was completely wrecked by the flood. He had problems reading and writing. As a consequence he was not able to get his place cleared and dried out as quickly as others. Judy and I helped him coordinate with the housing association and insurance as best we could. I also helped by giving him lifts to Gatehouse to see a lady friend in a nursing home there. He eventually got allocated a caravan till his flat was repaired. Sad to say that, in my absence working during the following year his health failed and he never made it back to his flat. Poor old soul. I sent flowers to the funeral. I spent a while getting the house in order and so that I could receive guests. This involved buying a lot of stuff on Amazon which was a good way of doing it. There are not many shops nearby. Once I got that resolved I started looking for work. I had been watching progress on the new Dumfries Hospital and thought this would be a good job for me. I had a meeting with a flooring contractor working there and agreed to start with them. I attended two days of induction. The day I arranged to start I met the contract manager on Site and was informed by the main contractor that our start would be delayed by two months. I told them I would probably have another job by then and that was end of that. Shortly after that I had an interview with an Irish firm who I had never heard of. There website showed that they had done a lot of work in Scotland and beyond during my time down south. I got an offer of a full time job on their new school in the region. On my first day I met the site engineer in the car park. He seemed a friendly chap. He took me to meet the Project manager who by contrast was not at all friendly. My first impression was correct and we never got on. I was soon transferred to another site. The people there were a bit more welcoming but the seed had been sown. My days were numbered. I carried on with my job. The contract manager always had an evil eye on me. I was released after 3 months trial. I never found out what the issue was. I suspect the Project Manager had other plans. He probably wanted to hire friends and family. That is quite common in the limited market here. I didn't see myself ever qualifying on these terms. My back was giving me trouble. To my surprise I found a Thai massage therapist nearby. The service was good and Dao was cheerful and friendly. I became a regular client. With her help I am able to continue strenuous walking, cycling, and swimming. I maintain a healthy life in my 60s. During this time Dao and I were close for a while. However it played on my conscience that she was married and I distanced myself. I often ask myself; why did I come back to Scotland? I am finding it hard to make a living. It always has been. But then I think this is my home. New York is not. San Francisco is not. I love the countryside. It's my home and I can do as I like. If it's not good for business learn to deal with it. Do other things. Don't worry what people think. Do your own thing. Do what you choose to do. You have the right to roam. Enjoy it. That's my new philosophy. I tend to keep getting dragged down by that Calvinist guilt they say exists in every Scot. I try to ignore that now. I am learning to speak my mind more and not worry about offending people. After all I'm always going to offend people I'm not fond of. I spent the last 40 years getting on my bike to work. A popular phrase coined by politicians in the 70s. That's enough thank you.

Western Isles. I had a phone call from an agency to say they had a contractor that would like to speak to me about an immediate start with a lot of hours. The job was in the Highlands. The contractor was based in Northern Ireland. I agreed to discuss it. In between times the agency informed me that the job was in the Western Isles and it was a refurbishment to a hotel. I did my homework; checked out the company website; Googled the hotel before the interview. They gave me some details about the job which was substantial £12Million. I told them what I had been doing. They had my CV and Portfolio. They said there were three jobs to consider. I made it clear I was interested in the Western Isles job. I had checked maps and knew the route which was a 4 or 5 hour drive from home and a 2 hour ferry crossing. I would be staying on site. The job appealed to me because it was in a remote location that I had not been to. I figured I would have a free hand as No 1 on site. I couldn't have been more wrong. I felt I did a good interview and got the job, we agreed terms. I started making arrangements to leave home. I would go to work for 2 or 3 weeks at a time returning for a long weekend. I enjoyed travelling there through stunning Highland scenery. I left early in the morning so I would arrive on site in the afternoon. The ferry was large and we had a good crossing. It was a sunny day and I spent most of the time on deck. It was truly spectacular. I got off the ferry and wound my way along the bumpy road to the site. I could see the hotel ahead of me. I pulled up at the site and met my contact for the first time. I wasn't sure what his role was. He explained to me that another man was meant to start the job. He decided not to after a week and had taken ill. He had been transferred to the site at short notice and would stay for a little while till I settled in. He said he was used to being a foreman on small jobs. This was too big for him. He was not good at IT or drawings. We had a cup of tea and a chat in the site office. He had started to set up in the few weeks he had been there. He took me out to see the site and meet the men. At that time there were several men establishing site. They were an amiable group from Ireland who all spoke with broad accents and expressions I was not familiar with. I had worked with many Irish in San Francisco and New York but these were a bit more home spun. My first impression of the hotel was that it was old and dilapidated. It probably should have been demolished. I also noticed that some work had been done before this contractor arrived. It was explained to me that another contractor did the enabling work. They did not win the main contract. My way of approaching a new job is to look and listen and respond politely. I keep my opinions to myself till I can figure out the whole picture. I was shown the accommodation. It was comfortable enough. The boss was coming to site the following day from N. Ireland to have a site meeting. My overall impression the first day was that their resources were limited. They were a bit behind the times of the construction industry in the UK That was ok. Not all the new ways are good ways. They were obviously hard working. Things could be improved. I was told that the firm were originally bricklayers of farming stock. They had gathered local tradesmen from Ireland around them. They had spotted a gap in the market for them in the Western Isles. The boss was a young very animated down to earth man. I had to concentrate hard to understand what he was saying. To me he sounded like a traveller. He was friendly enough but I soon learned that he only felt comfortable with his own folk around him. When he came on site he spoke directly to the men and ignored any protocols. This concerned me. I think it is important and good manners, that the Contract manager observes the hierarchy of management. A Site Manager cannot manage if he does not. I would give him the benefit of the doubt because it was a new relationship. Unfortunately this aspect did not improve but got worse over six months. They proved to be very parochial in their ways and this was not good for business. A project meeting was held shortly after I arrived and my hopes of this being a quiet little job on the Western Isles were dashed. The Project team was vast. I have never been a big fan of meetings. Yes they are necessary but when taken to a grand scale which this was it can defeat more than it achieves. The logistics of getting people there were sometimes difficult and expensive. The weather regularly affected these meetings in the winter and in addition to the monthly meetings we had additional meetings and conference calls. We had great difficulty getting good information during the first six months. Initially this was because the broadband was not connected. Once it was connected it was quite slow speed. It could only cope with 1 person using it. There was a huge quantity of drawings on site. On close examination the information was not complete or accurate. During my time on site we were constantly asking for more information to set out the buildings. I used this to the company's advantage to cover the fact that their resources were limited. Inevitably it made me enemies with the design team. What I did enjoy when I was there was the place itself. I used my spare time to explore the island fully on foot, bike, and car. The weather was forever changing but our location on dunes by the sea gave us some wonderful views of the weather, the light, and the changes. I enjoyed playing golf and swimming. I got on with the ground workers. I was enjoying the challenge of being a No1 on site. I was encouraging the men to work efficiently and keeping a close eye on the programme. I was fully aware we did not have the calibre or numbers of men we needed. I had been in this situation before and was an expert on maximising on limited resources. Where it fell down was that project teams ideas and my ideas of good practice were at odds. It was also annoying there were no bona fide contractors on work packages. This was making life easy for the men and harder for me. They could be an awkward bunch. I had to watch my back. The ground workers were doing a good job. They were constantly being criticised. They were not in the clic. As the job got busier a key trade was letting us down; the steel erector. The boss was probably the most ignorant man I have ever met. His work was terrible and he came to site when he felt like it. Because he was in the clic he seemed to get away with it. Despite my efforts we started to slip behind programme and there was nothing I could do about. I was aware criticism was building against me. The project team had meetings without me and decided to increase management on site. I knew given the circumstances this would not make a lot of difference. I got an assistant with less site experience than I was told and no qualifications. I spent a lot of time teaching him the ropes and making sure he went on the right courses. I was disappointed in him. He became part of the clic. Just before I left I was informed a new site manager would be joining us; the job should be split the into phases. When he arrived I didn't take to him. He was slightly younger than me, big earring, spoke like a traveller, came from Ireland and had been working in Nigeria. He had no qualifications, first aid or IT skills. I had met his sort before. They stabbed me in the back. One of the ground workers told me that the new man was saying he was here to replace me. We all sat in the meeting and I could sense the tide of change. I knew I would be working harder than ever teaching the new staff and trying to keep my head above water with this mutinous crew. My attitude was I have done 6 months on my own. You have more staff now. Sort yourselves out. My visits home usually coincided with the weekend. This suited me because the Thursday meetings could be exhausting. I must have had 6 visits home during my time there. It's fair to say that each time I went home I asked myself is it worth it? On 5 occasions I charged my battery sufficiently. I was drawn back. I always enjoyed travelling through Argyll. By the time I had done 6 months, I had enough. I did not believe in what they were doing. A good friend Bill had recently died and I had given notice that I would go home for the funeral. I went home the day after the meeting. Over the weekend I mulled over what to do. By Monday I had decided for certain. I was not going back, and quit. By now I was feeling ill. There had been a virus going round the site. I slowly recovered by the end of June. I have never been ill for so long. By now I had my fill of the building trade. I stopped pursuing jobs. I was never paid in full. I was warned this would happen.

Chapter 29 Penninghame Journal

Politically we are approaching a general election on **8 June 2017**. My experience has taught me not to follow traditional middle class values to choose who to vote for. My Mum & Dads middle class generation tend to vote Republican without reflecting on what has happened to them. For myself I have not voted much in my adult life because I believe there is an elite establishment; the civil service controlling people and political parties. It does not matter who you vote for. There are the haves and the have nots. When I first returned to Scotland I decided to take an interest in politics. I voted SNP who are strong in Scotland. I was impressed with Nicola Sturgeon but not Alec Salmond. Since then as this election was called 6 weeks ago I started to look at things again. I got involved in social media. I started to dislike Theresa Mays condescending way. Ever the underdog; I didn't like the fact she thought she was so far ahead in the poles she would win. She would carry on dictating to the electorate and serving the establishment and big business. People are looking for someone to serve them. I started to follow the Labour Party and Jeremy Corbyn. There was a movement on social media to encourage the young to take more interest in politics and vote. Now, 2 days before the election the poles are showing that Labour & Conservative are not far apart and I will vote for them. My only regret is that Labours fortunes in Scotland have been badly damaged by SNP. I now see the SNP as a distraction to UK politics. I see the electorate in Scotland as aspiring middle class. They do not want to be reminded of their working class roots. So they vote SNP or Conservative. Wrong. Neither serves Scotland well. My hope is that the young will take a different view and redress the balance in the UK by voting Labour. I firmly believe the ruling party should serve the people not dictate to them. I think they have this model in Australia for example. Foot note: Labour under Tony Blair was Conservative in disguise! In the Election, Labour, and Jeremy Corbyn surprised all but us tweeters, by gaining 30 seats. Conservative lost 15. It is a minority or hung parliament for Conservative with Theresa May probably fatally wounded. Labour and Jeremy Corbyn strengthened and on the up. During the campaign events in the UK came into play that shook the nation. Following the terrorist attack at Westminster where several lives were lost and many injured; there was a suicide bombing at Manchester Arena where a dozen lives were lost and many injuries at Ariane Grande concert. This was closely followed by an attack at London Bridge and Borough when 3 terrorists deliberately drove a van into pedestrians on the bridge followed by knife attack in Borough market. The police were better prepared on this occasion. The terrorists were wearing fake suicide vests with 12" ceramic knifes taped to their wrists. Again a dozen people were killed and up to 50 seriously injured. This was followed by a horrific fire at Grenfell Tower; a 26 storey residential tower block in West London occupied by poor ethnic minorities. 80 were killed and as many seriously injured. Serious questions being asked about fire safety and building methods. The building was destroyed very quickly and this building is similar to many others in UK. This event highlighted a generation of neglect. The building should have been safe. It was not. Reports highlighted a catalogue of neglect by government, civil service, institutions, and industry that caused these deaths. I think the young have been slow to grow up and take a roll in politics. It has taken the events of the last few weeks to bring them to the table. Social media is starting to galvanise the young in politics. It is a powerful tool. For many years the young felt they had no voice in politics. Tragedy and social media has given them that voice. I am encouraged to see that many support Labour policies.

Tuesday 20 June 2017. Sometimes I forget my life up till recently was in the USA. I had a dream. Last Friday I drove up to Fife in the VW by the A702 Galloway, Dalveen Pass, Biggar route. This is 1 of my preferred routes avoiding motorways these days. The scenery is spectacular in different ways. The Galloway Hills & forest, woodland, which becomes the brooding gloom of Dalveen Pass where one imagines many a man perished in Jacobite times. Into the heavy traffic of the Edinburgh bypass and the old Forth Bridge and a view of the new Queensferry Crossing now all joined up and due to open in the Autumn. On into Fife on the M90 and turn off for St Andrews & Dundee the weather has now turned from overcast to sunny blue skies and the rolling farmland of Fife around Auchtermuchty looking wonderful. On to Tayport and the magnificent views of Dundee, the Tay bridge, new development at the V&A, the docks and oil exploration platforms in for re fitting and down to Broughty Ferry and the castle and the beautiful Tay glistening in summer sun. Quick stop to buy a few essential supplies for my arrival at Doug's at 5 for dinner. I had just passed him in his Range Rover heading in Dundee direction. The house was open so I went in and dropped my things. I called as I went through the house to make myself known. Diane, Doug's youngest was upstairs and came down to greet me with a lovely smile and a peck on the cheek. She had heard yesterday she had graduated from university in fashion and I would hear later her plans to move to New York and try living and working there with her boyfriend Lee. We had a drink. Doug had gone to Dundee to pay the electrician who had wired lights in the garden. Kay was working. They would be home soon. I took a tour round the garden which was always interesting at Doug's. Following service in the Chicago Police Dept Doug became a landscape gardener and the garden was a thing of beauty. It was long garden, paths rambled over bridges, ponds, waterfalls, fire pits, various seating areas, Victorian lamp poles, down to the most amazing barbecue and a stone built bothy all amongst the most diverse and well-kept planting and a quarry pit at the bottom which would become a garage or accommodation in the future. Doug & Kay soon returned. After the usual greetings we had dinner and enjoyed the weather outside for the rest of the evening with some neighbours arriving for drinks. This went on till 2.30 am which is much later than I am used to. Too much whisky was drunk which I regretted the following day. Kay is a good host and enjoys a drink but sometimes I think it is more than good for us. If I had any plans for the following day, Saturday I didn't feel up to them. I got up late and as it was a nice day decided just to enjoy the garden. I had planned the trip for Father's Day Sun 18/6 and Dads 93rd birthday 19/6. Anyway a quiet day in the garden became a barbeque and friends and family. Including Dad & Eileen (Kays mum) who had been there the evening before. Recently since I returned from the Western Isles I have been spending a lot of time on my own. I find the company of many for an extended period, all afternoon and evening a bit much. As do Eileen & Dad. I was conscious of the fact I wasn't very sociable. In the evening after feeling uncomfortable at dinner, with my recent health problems, I excused myself. I fell asleep watching TV and went to bed at my usual 10.30pm. I was not fully fit after my recent illness. The following day Sunday, Father's Day I felt a lot brighter with the help of a hay fever pill which I suffer from recently. Kay and Doug had gone to a local car boot sale. I took advantage of the peace to have breakfast and wrap Dads present, "History of Flight" and "Old Malibu" and to contact Leyla & Bekka about lunch. I then phoned Jean to arrange to stay at hers that evening. Then I went down to Dad's with his present, and for a cup of tea. I left the door open because I knew Diane was having a lie in upstairs after a late shift at Pizza Express. Rocky the Border terrier was asleep in his favourite place in the Bothy. Dad now stays in a wee one bed flat 10 minutes' walk from Doug's. We had tea and lemon drizzle cake and he showed me his photos of planes he flew in the war and aircrew he shared his time with. It's amazing to think this wee old man was a US Navy pilot of the magnificent Catalina in 1944. What a hero. We watched the sparrows on the new bird table Jean bought him which is a shared interest of ours. I couldn't stay long as lunch was at 1 and I still had to go to get some essential provisions. Doug and Kay had got a few things at the boot sale including another lounger for the garden which was a bargain. It was another beautiful day. I picked up Dad and Eileen at 10 to 1. We all sat in the garden with a glass of Pimm's waiting for Leyla, Bekka and Jean to arrive. Jean was first to arrive with Millie the black Labrador who promptly plunged in the pond twice amongst the soup of pond life, frogs and tadpoles; emerging and shaking to shower anyone nearby. Jean had prepared pork and crackling for lunch. Leyla and Bekka arrived fashionably late with my Father's Day present, Aspall's Vintage Cider. They were looking very well; fashionably dressed; tattoos displayed I was not aware of. It amuses me to tally up how many and make an estimate of cost. They often claim to be broke. The conversation is about what the latest generation of McClains have been doing, many of whom are not with us. Diane is working at Pizza Express. Daniel & Ellie are in California, Jolene & Pat are in Banff, Canada. Rick newly married to … is planning to develop a hotel nearby. Ed is in the shipping business in Athens. Harry is in sales & marketing worldwide. Walt is in New York in Sales. Jim is in Frisco, soon to move to Glasgow. Leyla is enjoying working at Louisa, jewellery and gift shop new location. Bekka is enjoying modelling & marketing at "Little Lies" the web fashion brand. We had pate starters sat in the sun and then went inside for our main course and a delicious strawberry meringue pudding. After lunch we went back into the garden to enjoy the warm sunny weather and continue our conversation. After a while we dispersed. I was conscious of the fact that at Doug & Kay's an afternoon's pleasant escape could become a long evening party. I offered to take Dad and Eileen home at 5 o'clock. They accepted. By now they wanted to relax at home. . Leyla, Bekka and I bid Doug & Kay a fond farewell at 6 o'clock. I followed Bekka as far as the stables where I turned off to stay at Jean's for the night. I had to be careful going up the drive not to ground the car on the raised bit in the middle. The house was looking good following renovation. I carried on up to the cottage where I could see Jean had made a few improvements since my last visit. It was still warm and sunny. I had offered to cut the grass on the sit on lawnmower. At first I could not see anyone so I toured the cottage, yard and stables. I eventually found them at the reinstated ménage at the back where Jean and 2 livery friends were on horseback jumping. Millie greeted me with friendly barks coming through the garden. I watched them for a while and had a chat then set to work. Cutting the grass didn't take long on the sit on. Jill and I had time to sit out late in the evening, still warm and sunny. I could now relax and enjoy a cool glass of cider. In the morning after Jean had done her horse chores we went into town to see how Little Venice soon to become Milly's Kitchen was coming along. It was looking good. The previous dark tones had been replaced by more pleasing lighter tones in a more modern twist. We had to clear out the old kitchen fittings as the new equipment was on the way. After I went shopping for a pigeon proof bird feeder for Dads birthday today. We went to a nearby coffee shop. It was time for me to head to Glasgow to meet Jack. I said goodbye to Jean. She told me a way to go to Glasgow I hadn't thought of. Via Milnathort, Granny's former home Turfhills, Kincardine Bridge, now Clackmannan Bridge I wasn't aware of and so on to Glasgow. Jim texted me a postcode to meet him at 2.30pm. We had arranged to meet at the Ben Nevis, Argyll St, Finnieston. Jim was looking well. Glasgow life must be suiting him. We had a quick drink in the Ben Nevis which had a great selection of malt whiskies. We walked up and down this now trendy part of town to the Kelvin grove Gallery. We had a light lunch in the Firebird restaurant and headed into town about 5. I wanted to see the recent Billy Connelly mural at Hootenanny's beer garden. The actual paintings in the series of 3 by Vettriano, John Byrne, and … McLean are at the Peoples Palace, which is not open today unfortunately. We had a look and were impressed with the mural, and the sparrow that had made a nest in the wall at Billy's shoulder. I was struck with how sleazy central Glasgow was becoming. I can spot hookers and low life when I see them. It was getting late and I had a two and a half hour journey. I dropped Jim at his Tradeston apartment block. I was able to tell him it was not far from the Govanhill flat Daisy and I stayed with Leyla many years ago. It was close to the M77 (A77) to Ayr. I suggested to Jim he consider cycling to Malibu. And then I woke up. I have travelled too much in my life. My sense of time and place sometimes becomes confused.

Thursday 22/06/17 Some days I feel depressed. This is nothing new for me. I suffered when I lived in Chicago as a teenager. I have realised in the past that I have to keep myself active to avoid depression. It's the reason I left Chicago. It did not feel right at the time. Work wise and culturally. I felt I needed something different. It's the reason I kept returning to Frisco and the Big Apple. This time it's different. I am 60. This is my place and I am determined to find a way here. I have no other place and this is my last stand. I will just have to get on with it. I am worried about money. I have little income and little savings. I can fill my days with writing, gardening, reading, following things I like on TV and social media. I enjoy cycling, walking, exploring, and local history. I worry if I live as long as dad (93) that's 33 years. That's a long time to keep busy. Where's the money going to come from? I have decided the job I have always done, Site manager in construction, no longer has any appeal for me. Grenfell Tower killed any pride I had in the industry. So I am faced with trying to get a job simply for the money. I used to do construction for the challenge. Or should I do something else? I put my card in the newsagents. No response. But to be honest, I have not been answering the phone recently I'm not sure I want to do building at all. I have thought I might do something less demanding handyman, estate manager, housekeeper but I'm not sure. Or could I make a living from my writing? Any way the problem is I am not sure about anything at the moment. In the past I have been a positive person but I lost that in or around the Western Isles. I am sure I left for the right reasons. It doesn't make me feel any better. Yesterday I spent the morning cleaning up the laptop; 17 faults on the drivers. I was assisted by a nice woman in Manilla. I went to Kirkcudbright and spent an hour or so looking at the fishermen mending their nets. They use big metal frames that are dragged along the bottom collecting scallops; probably not good for the environment. Kirkcudbright is titled the Art Town. The shops are a mix of galleries, coffee shops, charity shops. None of which seemed very inspiring or lively to me in my darkening mood. I didn't have a coffee, or browse, or chat, or have fish & chips. I noticed it was a lovely day there. No disrespect to Kirkcudbright. I was having a bad day. I drove back my mood darkening. Ideas came and went. Big ideas dismissed. What to have for dinner, dismissed. I should have stayed at home watching Royal Ascot; dismissed. This is my problem at the moment; and of course the jackdaws. That's another story. When I got back to Penninghame I managed to make a positive decision to buy some provisions. I managed to raise a smile at the checkout. Little steps; watched the last 2 races at Royal Ascot. Big Orange win in the Gold Cup was a classic. I barely noticed and of course I hadn't backed it; always tomorrow. I hadn't noticed Royal Ascot was such a long meeting (till Saturday) eclipsed by Glastonbury, weather holding. Desert Island discs on radio 4 now. Jed Mercurio, Director of Line of Duty (Tandy Newton fav) talks to Kirsty Young. I didn't notice it was Thursday till I went to bed and read the" I" while listening to Annie Mac at Glastonbury. Up until then I thought it was Wednesday. I'm in a bad way. Did I mention the shift key doesn't always form a capital; that's annoying? I have been reading too much "The Art of Failure" Goodnight.

Friday 29/06/17. Yesterday I arranged to collect Dad from Hamilton services. Doug was going to drive him there. He was due to come here for 4 nights while his flat was cleaned. I was on route as far as New Galloway when I got a call from Dad to say he had to abort the journey due to Eileen (Kay's mum)taking ill. I tried to contact Doug but he was too preoccupied to provide me with information. I went home to await further instructions in the morning. Dad was very disappointed. I knew that Eileen was in hospital to have a tumour removed from her head. I could only surmise that complications had arisen. Eileen is 80 and quite frail. This caused me to think of spiritual matters. Kay a lifelong catholic has in recent years rejected faith following reading a book she gave me but have not read. I have a faith but not in the sense that I am a Church of Scotland protestant who regularly goes to church. I believe in a greater power that influences our lives. I believe this power also influences nature and animals. I believe animals understand things. Good and evil for example. Different faiths consider other faiths good or evil on a rating system. I take aspects of for example

Christian, Hindu, Muslim, Buddhist, Jewish faith as part of my faith. I care for animals but I don't like Jackdaws and Crows. I think they have a mobbing nature that I don't like so I don't encourage them. I don't like Tories. To me there is badness about them. Nowadays it is difficult to define who and what people are. As a nation we like to stick a label on people if we can. This is becoming difficult. However prejudice still exists. I have just come off the phone to Dad who told me Eileen died last evening at 9pm. Bless her. Now I would wait for news when the funeral is and bring Dad here on my return from the funeral. Doug has not been in contact to tell me the circumstances of her death. I believe she went to a hospital appointment yesterday to have a tumour removed from her head.

Sunday 2 July 2017. Yesterday I could see on my BBC Phone app that it would be sunny in the morning and dark in the afternoon and so it was. Nowadays I am slow to get ready to go out. Asthma and hay fever trouble me these days and it takes me a while to get going. Yesterday I got up and was out at Glentrool by 9.15am. It was a bit of a struggle and I felt a bit out of sorts but I was here with my trustee bike and ready to go. I am in the habit of doing the big country trail in 3 different ways. 1. From home along Wood of Cree road to Stroan Bridge Forestry Commission coffee shop and back after coffee and a scone. 2. From home across George V Suspension Bridge up the Cumloden Road and Old Edinburgh Rd and back home. 3. Take the bike in the car to Glentrool coffee shop car park. From there, head to Bruces Stone; and onwards to the Big Axe stone at Loch Dee. These 3 stretches are fabulous mixes of scenery and demands on me and the bike. I do an hour and a half out and an hour and a half back. This is good exercise for a man of my mental and physical instability. It's all part of the Big Country Trail which if you are feeling ambitious you can do as one complete circuit of 34 miles up and down dale. I have an advantage on Grandad. I can cover more ground on my bike, on the newly established forest roads of Galloway. His advantage was that he would walk and stop, and think and notice things, that you only notice when you dander. He had time to dream in the fabulous remoteness of the Galloway Hills. As I write, I look out the window and see a fine specimen of a Great Spotted Woodpecker clinging to the concrete washing post at the bottom of the garden. This post is becoming the VIP suite of my bird feeding club. Only rarity's come here. Previously I had seen a nuthatch. This is my club. Sparrows, blue tits, great tits, coal tits, gold crests, chaffinches, blackbirds, wood pigeons, pheasants are welcome. Jackdaws and cats are not. I am the doorman. They cannot come in. Sometimes I worry about my mental state!

Tuesday 4 July 2017. Woke up about 6am and noticed my breathing was obstructed and my throat was clicking as I breathed. I had taken a Benadryl yesterday lunchtime and decided to try 1 first thing this morning and 2 puffs of my brown inhaler. It was raining and I had to put the bin out early. By now I could tell it was 1 of these days where I could not imagine myself doing a full time job. Recently since I returned from the West I suffer in the same way my mother did at my age of unspecific illness. I have mostly good days but a few bad days. I don't feel well enough to leave the house till at least lunchtime. I have explored the symptoms with the 10 minutes doctors can afford the public these days, but no solutions offered. As the morning progresses, my breathing difficulty becomes nausea and dizziness. I try to self-diagnose to no avail. Could this be a symptom of depression? Get out and get busy. Don't feel up to that. Change your life to allow for the illness. It's only going to get worse. You'll get no sympathy because it's not like a broken leg. There is a Yiddish theory that the age of 60 is the start of a new phase of life. "Mensch" Perhaps one should put all that went before aside and see where the future takes you. Thinking about it from the age of 0 to 30 you are absorbing all that is put before you and making something of it."Schlepper" But you have little choice about what you see particularly when you are at school. In the age of 30 to 60 you are applying what you learnt previously to the best of your abilities. "Macher" Men are probably programmed in the 1st life to provide for their family in the 2nd life. This is their priority. The 3rd life from 60 to death is before me and I do not have a desire to continue what I did in the 2nd life i.e. working as a Site manager and providing for my family. My aims for my 3rd life are more selfish, creative, and based on a greater understanding of the world around me. I still have grand ambitions. I don't know where I am going. I have never been this way before.

5 July 2017. I am feeling better this morning. I did not go out at all yesterday other than to bring the bin in. It rained all day. The Tour de France which takes place for most of this month has caught my interest. Full coverage is on TV. Mark Cavendish crashed yesterday breaking his arm when Peter Sagan elbowed him into the barrier at the finishing sprint. Sagan was disqualified then reinstated. Chris Froome wears the yellow jersey, Bahrain Merida in the mix on day 3. Wimbledon day 3: It is being commented on that several players have retire injured. Questions are being asked whether they were fit to play a full game. It has been suggested that they started for the money. This can be as much as £75000 for starting the game. Spoke to Doug yesterday. Eileen's funeral planned for Monday. I will drive to Dalkeith and bring Dad home for a 4 day break. I need to get out today.

Saturday 8 July 2017. I could see on the weather app it was going to be a sunny afternoon. I got myself organised to go on a hike to Loch Middle. You can get to Loch Middle by walking through Wood of Cree. Over the gate to Cordorcan Bothy and beyond; On forestry roads for 2-3 miles following the Pulhonan Burn. The walk through Wood of Cree is lovely. An ancient oak wood; cut down for the 1st World War effort. The wood is returning now. There are lovely stretches of burn to see. There are many species of birds here. Beyond the wood is quite desolate. Once or twice I looked over my shoulder. The wind rushed through the conifers. Many trees have been blown over, uprooted, in distressed wreckage, domino effect, of fierce wind, and rain. As I had not been here before it seemed further than it looked on the map. I checked my OS Locate against map & compass just to check I was on route. As is often the case some of the forestry roads were not on the map. As I walked I thought of places nearby called Pinkies Hole, a cave. A fictional character my grandfather had written about. Silver Rig; Site of abandoned silver mine. Thinking, I must go and visit to see if there is still silver there. Eventually I could see Loch Middle shimmering blue in the sunlight ahead of me. I was beginning to think I would have to turn back. It had taken longer than I thought. I had been walking slowly and stopping regularly to look at things. I could see a stone wall undamaged by "the Levellers" making its way from the loch up Punch Well Brae through Black Gairy to Larg and Lamachan. I have been looking recently for a suitable ascent of Lamachan and just by chance I found one. This is often the case. It looked like the hardest bit would be a steep, short stretch where the dyke went through the conifers. A big healthy fox ran across my path. That's a surprise. A fox ran across my path yesterday but previously I have not seen a fox since I returned to Galloway. Is it a sign? When I got to the loch I could see a sign put up by Scottish Water to say the loch was a water source. I'm guessing for surrounding farms and maybe Glentrool. As I stood by the water's edge I saw a buzzard wheeling around on the far side of the loch. It was coming my way in slow circles so I stood quietly to observe it. I had binoculars in the bag but sometimes it's best to stay still and observe without them. As it came closer and I saw its white underside I thought that's not a buzzard. It was the size of a big buzzard but sleeker with a white underside patrolling the loch. I thought it's an Osprey. I could see it had a mate in the distance above the trees on the far side. It came as close as overhead not too high and didn't seem concerned by my presence and then headed back towards its mate. I was convinced it was an osprey when I heard it call *ee* a short call compared to the *eeeweee* repeated of the buzzard. Well that made my day. What should I do? A rare sighting, I thought about it as I had a sandwich by the loch. It looks like a lake, Should I tell RSPB or keep it to myself. I don't want its beauty spoiled by a radio tag. I set off back to the car park. As I turned to leave there was a big swirl of water in the reeds near the edge. I had been watching dragon flies I had not seen on previous outings, fluorescent blue and fat brown ones. The swirl was a large fish, maybe a pike or a trout or could it be an otter. I hadn't been quick enough to see. But proof that it was good fishing for an Osprey. After some thought, I contacted the RSPB. They emailed me back to say there had been reports of Ospreys fishing in the nearby, Cree. No reports of where I had seen them. However the same pair could be fishing the Cree. They would investigate.

Friday 14/07/17. Yesterday I was writing about my relationship with Sophia and as I wrote I realised that I had forgotten something. We had two splits during our relationship. This reminded me that following my split from Lily I resolved not to enter a relationship again. My marriage and all of my relationships have ended acrimoniously. I have to take responsibility for this. I admit that I am not successful at long term relationships. I am uncompromising. The same applies in the workplace. I start with great enthusiasm. If I am lucky a job or assignment can last for 5 years. Recently though I have seen imperfections in the set up early. That leads to me leaving after 6 months. What next? I am now 60. What are my options? Stay as I am. Not getting involved in relationships and work?

Monday 24/07/17 Start of another week. I have now written 135 pages, 57,000 words of my journal. Once I got started. I adopted my own style. I always write in the morning. I spend about 3 hours writing each morning. I find I can immerse myself in it. Writing is a big improvement on what I knew before. There was depression. The start of the day was difficult. I look forward to it now. In the past this has been "going to work". Writing gives me a way of recording and validating my life. Eventually I assume I will suffer from loss of memory. The means to do this will be gone for ever. I sometimes get frustrated in company that I can't get a word in. The beauty of writing is you are not competing to have your say. I have also satisfied an ambition. To finally do what Grandfather did. The other great unknown is my writing worthy of a readership. I am getting to a stage now when the end is in site of the first draft. I will read it through to add names I have forgotten and add bits I missed. My aim was to write a piece that was the length of a novel 90,000 words. I am falling short of this. However I am now reading a novel in one sentence Solar Bones by Mike McCormack which is 265 pages, 63,600 words. It's all a matter of where you draw the line. The other question is FICTION. Can I make the leap from my journal to fiction or do I continue my Journal and go in depth in certain areas. Yesterday I went for a walk. I wanted to watch the Finale of the Tour de France, Chris Froome's imperious return to Paris. His fourth win. I have been following le Tour closely for the last 3 weeks. I also want to see the Final day of The Open and the battle between Jordan Speith and Kuchar. I wanted to walk up the stretch of the Minnoch described in Grandads Chapter Otter Hunting in Galloway in Words from the Wild Wood, illustrated by John Copland. I started and followed the Southern Upland Way track from Brigton Wood until I could see High Minniwick and Dalane Cottage on the other side of the footbridge at Water of Minnoch. It was one of those solitary walks where I tend to look over my shoulder from time to time. Wind in the trees. In places the fern was as tall as me. You drive through it confidently. Thinking of stories you have heard of adders liking this space. Or times you startle yourself by raising a deer or a pheasant. In Grandads story the 30 hunters, followers and hounds hunted the otter from the Cree at Larg to where the burn meets Loch Trool. As I walked I thought the hunt was surely in winter when the water was flowing slowly after a dry spell. To negotiate this stretch in a large group would be impossible. The fern was high almost obscuring the path completely in many places. The burn was a raging torrent after the recent rain. The hunting party would have been swept back to the Cree or drowned. As I write a nuthatch is perched on the nut feeder upside down having a feed. By the time I reached the footbridge to High Minniwick I realised I had taken longer than I intended. It was 3.00pm and I could feel rain in the air. The path had been slippy in places where there was ground water. The rain would make it worse. By the time I got back to the Pug and fired it up there was spots of rain on the windscreen. I went back by Wood of Cree listening to a bit of jazz. I looked for the path to the disused Silver Mine at Silver Rig as I passed Cordorcan but I couldn't see it. Silver panning in the burn can wait.

Monday24/07/17 I started the day writing. It was a sunny morning with blue skies. The weather app said it would remain sunny all day till evening. There was something I had not done for a while. This would be **"Merrick Monday"** The conditions were perfect. One of the great advantages of being semi-retired in Penninghame is that I can pick the best days for hill climbing. I already had my stuff ready from yesterday so I was parked and ready to go at Bruce's Stone parking by noon. There were a number of cars there. Other people had the same idea. I set off and it soon became apparent that the path up the Buchan Burn is as bumpy as I remembered it. In wet weather the path is a natural route off the hill for ground water and all the fines, the grit and small stones are washed out leaving large boulders you have to hop one to the other. You have to concentrate and be quite agile. The last thing you want is to turn an ankle when you're on your own. There are accounts of climbing the Merrick in Grandads "Galloway The Spell of its Hills & Glens" I suspect it was not like it in his day. He was in the habit of climbing the Merrick. He did so on his 80th birthday. I am a slow walker. I often stop to take in the view and let other walkers go by. I am not fond of a group with a fast walker leading the group. Some people are quite competitive about walking. Not me. I reached the Culsharg bothy which I was pleased to see was in better condition than last time. It had been swept and cleared ready for the next weary souls. One sad aspect of the extensive de forestation is that there is little wildlife in evidence. They prefer quieter spots. The Forestry Commission who are soon to have a name change to Forestry Scotland have fenced and planted a large area here and planted traditional varieties of Juniper, Aspen, Birch that have been lost. The path from the bothy through the forest to the hill is steep and again ground water has washed it out making it a tough ascent. Once on the hill the path is maintained and the gradient steepens as you climb to the cairn on Benyellary 719 . Recently I have found I don't have the puff for steep ascents and I find it beneficial to put my head down and count stretches of 300 paces then stop for a breather; or 100 paces if it's steep. Admire the view then push on. It seems to help. To the unaccomplished you think you have reached the top, but look on beyond. Is that summit not higher? It is. The path goes on and down and up the Nieve o the Spit and the Scars to the Merrick 843 the highest peak in Galloway. I touched the Trig Point as tradition at 3pm. Some people put a new stone on the cairn. There was a few up there scattered in sheltered spots on the top. The views were at their finest today. Clear views West to the coast Ailsa Craig, Paddy's Milestone, Arran, and Ireland beyond; up North to central Scotland and Glasgow; down South, to the mountains of the Lake District; and East to the Borders. Some say you can see Snowdon on a clear day but I didn't try on this occasion. There are many wind farms to see in all directions. Thankfully pressure from nature lovers and lovers of Galloway, the Scottish Mountaineering Society and RSPB has legislated that they are far on the horizon of the Galloway Hills on what I call the scrub hills of Ayrshire, Lanarkshire and the coast. The sky today was beautiful to photograph, blue sky with little scatterings of wispy cloud. It's worth walking in a wide circle around the summit to take in the varying ascents to the summit and plan future routes. The view of Little Spear is spectacular and Lochs Enoch, Arron, Neldrickon, and Valley with rugged Craignaw behind are alternative ways back if you are feeling energetic via Redstone Rig. I chose to descend the way I had come. The condition of the path is poor in places. There is more risk of injury on the descent. Lactic acid has by now deserted you. Many places require concentration and a bit of agility to avoid injury. By now the legs and feet are feeling the pain. By the time you get to the point where the higher path goes down to the lower path you'll be ready for a taxi but there's still boulders and hops to negotiate on your weary legs. I was grateful to reach the Pug and loosen my boots and remove grit just before 6pm. Note to self. See what can be done to improve the path from Bruce's Stone to the Bothy. It's a heartbreaker! And home for a warm bath to try and revive this old body.

I noticed when I got on the scales 3 weeks ago after a night in the pub that I was well on the way to 15 stone. I could feel my clothes straining round my middle. I decided to go on a diet. I had read recently that the Jacobite's when fighting in Europe on the Crusades for the Stuarts lived on oats. They were reputed to be strong fighters and marchers. This is my diet.

The Jacobite Diet (Not)

I have recently done some research and found my allegiance is to the Galloway Levellers and Covenanters. Not the Jacobites. This is their diet! I have also included tips from pro cyclists. (Rice cakes)

Breakfast: Tea, porridge with banana, honey, semi skimmed milk. I now make this in the Nutribullet with whey protein. As recommended by Beaumont, the record breaking round the world cyclist. He did the journey in less than 80 days recently.

Coffee

Lunch, diced carrots, celery, Ryvita, oatcakes, humus, taramasolata, Activia, juice (Nutribullit)

Coffee, Fig roll

Dinner, tea, Activia, fig roll

Supper, Milk, digestive biscuit, fig roll

Alcohol allowed three days a week. Combine this with regular strenuous mountain biking, walking, and swimming. To date I am now at 13.5 stone.

Monday 31 July 2017. It is the end of July. May was our Summer, June and Julys weather has been a bit mixed. I have had to keep a close eye on the weather. I have picked my moments for gardening, mountain biking, enjoying sun and warmth. I have finished the first draft of my scribblings. Putting your thoughts on paper is a good thing to do. It is a good record. The act of writing forces you to put these into a form of communication. Putting it out there is another thing altogether. Do you want other people to know personal things? Things you regret. Controversial matters. There is a feeling that you want to have some sort of validation for your work. My Grandfather wrote several books. I have always found this fascinating. Before I started I saw it as a challenge to see if I could write. If I could sit down day after day putting words on the page until I had produced something I could call a novel. I found that after an uncertain start it got easier for me. I can sit down and lose myself in my writing. Before I started writing, I would not know what to do with the start of the day. Now, writing starts the day and the rest comes more naturally and positively.

Thursday 27 July 2017 I went to Edinburgh for the day. I was starting to get cabin fever which I think everyone who lives here experiences from time to time. I wanted to see the "Bonnie Prince Charlie and the Jacobite's" and the "Galloway Hoard" exhibitions which were on at the National Museum of Scotland in Chamber Street at the same time. I drove to Lockerbie in the VW and caught the 10am train to Edinburgh arriving at 11. I was a bit early so I went to Greggs for a coffee and a bacon roll "wi broon sas." Delicious. I decided to break my diet as I was having a day out. I walked up to the museum via Cockburn Street and George IV Bridge. The Old Town. At a time when Bristol is changing the names of the city out of respect for former slaves on whom the city was founded. I am surprised Edinburgh has not followed suit in respect of the persecuted Scots of the past. Both exhibitions were excellent. The Galloway Hoard reminded me of the Detectorists on TV. What must it be like to find such a hoard. It was of 9th 10th Century Viking origin worth at least £1Million, discovered by Ayrshire detectorist Derek McLennan in September 2014. He was searching on undisclosed Church of Scotland land in Dumfries & Galloway. The Jacobite exhibition was a fantastic display of the events around the times of the Royal Stuarts (Stewarts, Stewards) which I have just finished reading. I was struck by the passion raised amongst the Jacobites by Bonnie Prince Charlie. He spent most of his life in exile in France. It reminded me of the short lived fame of a modern day celebrity. Did he give the various King Georges and the current Hanoverian Royals great cause for concern? It's quite amusing that Rod Stewart the pop star was recently honoured with a Knighthood at Buckingham Palace. By Prince William the Hanoverian who will be King. Rod was dressed in a modern day Jacobite Stewart tartan, a difficult moment for the future King. My feet were getting sore walking round the museum. I will return. I took out membership. I walked round to Victoria Street. I was struck by how many more tourists there are in Edinburgh now. Tourism seems to have taken over from the traditional administrative and commercial activity. I was pleased to sit down in the Bow Bar. In a previous life I have used this place as a satellite office. I enjoy a glass of Edinburgh cider and a steak pie and gravy. Some tourists at the bar were enjoying a tasting session of the beers on tap. In the past that would not happen. The barmaid yawned. I then went to Greyfriar's Church yard where I had learned I could see the Covenanters Jail. I was directed to old Wullie in the church. I recognised the church as the place I had been many years ago for Jock and Ellie's wedding. Wullie was pleased to have a break from large groups of young tourists on the Hawwy Potta tour to give me a personal tour of the jail. He unlocked the 17th century gate to show me the yard where 1200 Covenanters were incarcerated awaiting there trial and grisly fate. Many tombs of eminent people of Edinburgh can be seen in the graveyard. Wullie told me if the stone featured skull and crossbones, many do, it means the occupant was a freemason. It started to rain. Wullie pointed me in the direction of the Magdalene Chapel. I passed the stone on route which described the Covenanters fate. The chapel was founded by the incorporation of Hammermen, for all trades who use a hammer in their work. I guess I would qualify as a carpenter. During the persecution of the Covenanters, following execution in the Grassmarket there bodies or body parts laid on a table that is still there. They were dressed in grave clothes and laid to rest in Greyfriars Church Yard. I caught the 4 o'clock train from Waverley station to Lockerbie. By the time I drove back to Penninghame it was 6.30pm. Winston with Brian Cox was on at the cinema but I decided to see it another time.

Wednesday 2 August 2017 Wigtown Show is on today but it's wet. I can't make up my mind whether to go today or another year when the weather is better. I went along and it was wet but fun. Good displays and performances by Monster Trucks, Sheep Beauty Contest & Shearing Show, Show Jumping, Poultry, Livestock, Show Jumping, Crafts, Local Produce, Farm Machines & Vehicles, and much more. I bought a bottle of Hills & Harbour gin at great expense and some local pies. David and Graeme were promoting Crafty, Newton's new distillery. I was completely soaked by the time I found the car and set off for home.

Sunday 6/08/2017. Art phoned me on Friday with the sad news that Shymie had died. I met Shimmy in 1998 or 1999. She had just met Ian at the Nova Scotia. We were all recovering from upheavals in our lives. We banded together to live in fragile harmony. Despite our difficulties we started to live again. This was largely due to Shimmy's enthusiasm for life. She looked back on her life, and forward to the future with equal enthusiasm.

Tuesday 15 August 2017. I am being the dutiful son by having my Dad to stay for 4 days. He is 93 and I have been brought up to respect my elders. I shall try to be the perfect host. I shall stoically go about my duties and put him on the train on Friday with a wave and a grimace. I hope I don't live so long. It is difficult. Perhaps grandchildren would give me a new lease of life.

Friday 18 August 2017. Following Dads visit to Penninghame I wrote a letter to his doctor. I sent it to Doug & Jean instead as they lived closer to him. They are his guardians.

Dear Sirs,

Re: Andrew Neill McClain, Age 93

I have spent the last week in the company of my Dad, Neill.

I have sadly come to the conclusion that he is now suffering from senility or senile dementia to the extent that he requires a daily health visitor. I speak as a lay man. His father Andrew died at the age of 90 with what was then described as senility. The symptoms came to my attention when I went into the kitchen. It was infested with flies. I gave it a deep clean and noticed signs of eccentric behaviour that were causing the infestation. He was storing banana skins and food containers. This had not come to the attention of his meals on wheels delivery person as they never entered the kitchen. I advised the young man when I saw him it was a good idea that he did. Incidentally he would prefer to have vegetarian meals delivered in future. He recently had a letter to say he would benefit from a vaccination. He has not made an appointment because he could not make himself understood to the receptionist. A daily health visitor would be able to monitor him to ensure he is comfortable and not at risk. He needs to be reminded about hygiene, haircuts, changing his clothes daily and cleaning them. He has a few moles, skin lesions that need dressing, treating. I think he manages well on his own but just needs a bit of daily support. I have noticed that as much as you tell him things, he reverts back to the same behaviour the following day. Family are nearby to add additional support. Doug & Jean (his children) have power of attorney over his affairs. I would like to do more but I am by nature not a carer. I live 150 miles away and I am sorry to say would not be patient enough to care for him daily.

Kind regards,

AJ McClain

Sunday 20 August 2017 I have been saying for some time now that I would return to work in October and work for six months till March. I have to take account of my age and health. My chosen job as a Site Manager in construction can be demanding, physically and mentally. It is sometimes not a healthy environment. I recently had a letter from the NHS requesting I make an appointment to see an Occupational Therapist. What is my current state of health? Summarising,

Eyesight: Short sighted. I have to wear glasses to read technical plans. Out on site this can slow you down, particularly in bad light or bad weather. For the last 25 years I have occasionally suffered from blurred peripheral vision. (Ocular Migraine) This takes 10 minutes to clear if I rest, close my eyes, or put on dark glasses. It is sometimes accompanied by a feeling of weakness, nausea. It is not said to be harmful.

Hearing: Not as good as it was. I suffer from tinnitus which is getting louder. I hear a continuous high pitch noise.

Balance: Not as good as it was. I suspect this is affected by a build-up of wax in the ear canal. I use olive oil and ear candles to help with this. When I look above me or at my feet I feel giddy for a moment. I wonder if this is a trapped nerve in my neck.

Breathing: In recent years I have become shorter of breath. I take medication for asthma when I have too. Following my last work assignment I did not feel in full health for 2 months. I put this down to a virus I picked up on site. This left me with a cold and a cough. It became sinusitis which was accompanied by a persistent headache every day. I took paracetamol daily for 2 months. I have an inhaler for asthma. I have a nasal spray for sinusitis.

Digestion: I suffer from GORD or reflux. Certain foods start a reaction like a valve closing in my throat, beef, bread, and beer. I have changed my diet to avoid this happening. I now follow the Levellers Diet. The diet is vegetarian and based on porridge oats which I make into a smoothie in the NutriBullet with banana, oats, whey protein, honey and milk. I also eat diced carrot, celery, fruit juice and Activia. My health has improved and my weight is stable at 13.5 stone.

Blood pressure: This has been on the high side for at least 25 years. Blood pressure is 85 over 135 on average, and heart rate 55bpm.

Note added Tue 14/11/17. My health has improved dramatically since I became vegetarian and follow the Levellers Diet.

General health: I continue to hill walk, mountain bike and swim regularly for pleasure. This helps to maintain a good level of fitness in spite of the problems I have summarised.

Returning to work, taking into account my current state of health, age 61 on the 30 September 2017. My chosen job Site Manager for 30 years is probably not a good choice now. A No 1 on a modern site is operating under a considerable amount of stress in a hostile environment. The workforce now is a much younger generation. They are not as able to read and understand technical information, plans as tradesmen in the past. They demand information quickly from the No 1 constantly. I prefer to work at my own pace nowadays. Perhaps I should now be looking for a role that does not manage the workforce directly. Has no responsibility for enforcing Health & Safety, a role that uses my experience and knowledge, Project Management, inspection, technical support. Or perhaps I should do something different.

23 August 2017 Well that appears to be the end of the school holidays. The weather since May has been a bit mixed to be kind. We have been getting a lot of low cloud. There is generally a period of 2 or 3 hours each day when it's a little bit sunny to get out for a walk or a cycle. I am preoccupied with my future. How will I make a living? Writing? My Journal is up to date. I planned to go on to write fiction. I thought about an epic novel of a family, this family in fiction. Going back to the 17th century, developing from being farmers, to smugglers, to Jacobite soldiers fighting the Hanoverians, Covenanters fighting for their chosen life, religion, and monarchy, and how each generation changed up to the present day and beyond to survive in their particular generation. The ups and downs in fortune; the need to emigrate to America; Canada, Australia, and New Zealand. How farmers became smugglers, dealers, soldiers, professionals, builders, artists. I have written American Dream 1955 - 2020. I am thinking about publishing. Work wise I have more or less decided that it's not a good idea to go back to being a Site Manager. My age, health, and lack of enthusiasm for the work lead me to this conclusion. When I read job boards I think. I don't like the look of that or that. The small amount of savings I have will go and then what.

Tuesday 29 August 2017 Excitement is growing now for the opening of the Queensferry Crossing tomorrow. Leyla, Bekka and I have tickets won in the ballot to be amongst 50,000 pedestrians from 250,000 who applied to walk over the new bridge on Saturday. More to follow.

I have spent a lot of time recently reading about the history of Penninghame district in Wigtownshire and the surrounding parishes. In particular, the period of 1600s and 1700s. I managed to trace the Family Tree back to the 1750s but the period of the Jacobite Rebellions and the Covenanters is more difficult to follow. I spent a day in Edinburgh at the museum and Greyfriar's Church and Magdalene Chapel gathering some valuable information. After that I came across a dissertation by Alastair Livingston for his M. Phil (Research) in History 2009 titled The Galloway Levellers.

This was an invaluable piece of research, well written. My overall impression of this period was that it was very interesting, complex, influential to this day, locally and beyond, in the wider world. We have religion, the crown and the clans playing a major role in how the parish of Penninghame lived and developed. We have conflict during the period for the crown between the Jacobites and the Hanoverians. On a local level the Stewarts (or Stuarts) from Newton Stewart or more accurately Garlies North of Minnigaff. The church has a strong influence. There were many divided loyalties at work. Some landlords were protestants, covenanters with a strong mistrust of catholics and loyal to the Hanoverian throne. Some landlords were Catholics, with Jacobite loyalties sometimes referred to as "Papish Gentlemen" To add to the mix the clans had different loyalties according to history. Tenants were sometimes loyal to their landlord but not always. Galloway's proximity to Ireland as a trade route was also very influential.

Protestants	**Catholics**	**Clans**	**Crown**
Tenants	Landlords	Stewart	James
Covenanters	Jacobites	Maxwell	Charles
Levellers	Papish Gentlemen	Murdoch	
			George
Presbyterians	Episcopalians	Heron	Hanoverians
		Nicholson	Windsors
		Murray	
		McConnell	
		McDowall	
		Kennedy	

During the 1600's and 1700's there was a move by landlords to evict tenant smallholders from the land by increasing rents. The landlords were keen to form large "cattle parks" in Wigtownshire and Kirkcudbright. Both counties were on the cattle trade route from Ireland to England and Central Scotland. This was despite the trade from Ireland being illegal. The landlords were building dry stone dykes to keep cattle in and demark their land. The tenants were suffering by rent increases, eviction and change of land use. They formed a large protest movement based in Kirkcudbright known as the Galloway Levellers. They expressed their unhappiness at the change in land use by damaging dykes that were being built and slaughtering Irish cattle housed therein. The cattle parks were never fully established largely due to the tenants protest.

Having read about this period in history I can understand how mistrust was established in the region between different classes, religions, clans, royal and political allegiances. These feelings were established at a time when many suffered and died unjustly. I can understand if people have strong feelings today originating from their surname and family history.

As I sit by the window writing it's difficult to concentrate due to the theatre of birdlife in the garden. My reward for spending 6 months at home is that my garden is now a haven for all the birds from the wood at the end of the garden to eat a the 2 feeders I have hanging from the washing line. Yesterday it was too wet all day to restock the feeders as I usually do on a Monday. I had to wait till evening when the birds had retired to the wood to do it. As time goes by the birds get to know that I stock it on a Monday only. I do this because the seeds in particular disappear in a couple of days. If I was to refill it immediately the birds get too fat. So they do without seeds till Monday. I have battled to keep unwelcome guests such as jackdaws, cats, dogs away and I feel I am beginning to win. Today I have the following in pecking order,

Great spotted Woodpecker

Nuthatch 3 No

Great Tit 3 No

Blue Tit 5 no

Coal Tit 3 No

Robin 2 No

Sparrow 15 no

Bullfinch 3 No

Bunting/brambling 8No

Swallow 5 No

Blackbird 3 no

Thrush 3 no

I have a greater respect for birds since I heard they evolved from dinosaurs. It makes sense to me. When they were great lumbering beasts survival was difficult. As birds flight is a better option for survival than fight. I can see dinosaur in a heron for example.

6 September 2017. If I did not know before why this place, this Wigtownshire, this Kirkcudbright is known as "Grey Galloway" I do now. The sky has been heavy with grey cloud, low, clutching the hills, releasing rain at regular intervals. Everything is damp, saturated. There is a smell of saturated vegetation. Slugs and other ground living creatures thrive. It has been like this for 6 weeks, maybe more. There was a promise of summer in May. It never came to anything. Living here is a challenge. In the modern world there is an expectation that we be happy, fulfilled, and entertained. Where did this expectation come from? When I think about it I think it probably came from TV, the media in the seventies. Colour television gave us an expectation of colourful lives. Television gave us glamorous people with a ready smile and a happy demeanour. As TV developed it all became more. Better televisions, more colour, bigger, better sound. The media became more accomplished. What we saw on our screens became what we call normal. We started to be what we saw on TV. The world is now full of colourful people with a ready smile and a happy demeanour. This is less so in "Grey Galloway" In sunny May when visitors come it seems like heaven. Visitors have dreams of living in this lovely place. They look in estate agents windows and dream of a happy new life. If they stay longer, particularly this year, they will have cause to think twice. The ready smiles of residents and visitors alike become more strained. "Grey Galloway" requires a different approach. The weather is everything here. Your personality mirrors the weather, you have to accept that. To put on a sunny disposition in the certainty of the greyness seems false and unsettling. The greyness encourages a melancholy disposition, a humble acceptance of nature's superiority. Those used to the everyday sunny disposition of other places will suffer or flee. Those of us who stay and have lived other lives adapt or suffer. We become more aware of the weather, the seasons, dawn, dusk, the position of the sun, the moon. Nature, animals can help by teaching us how to live here. You have to change your mental state from being demanding to being accepting. If your life is not structured make it so. If you do not "Grey Galloway" will get you. You will become dour, eccentric, dull, depressed or variations thereof. Faith is a comfort for some. Companionship, family is the salvation of many.

Monday 11 September 2017 Children have returned to school, swallows have flown to Africa, politicians have returned to Parliament from summer retreats, this immaculate timetable, that brings such certainty and contentment to many, a sense of inevitability, worthiness. Worry, fear dispelled. Not for me. An uncertain future has always been part of my life.

Like a bottle of whisky beckoning to the alcoholic. Take me.

You know you shouldn't but here I am. Take me.

Do the Blessed experience this gnawing fear.

Did they feel it once and think, never again.

Stick to the immaculate timetable, for beyond lies Bedlam, madness.

Busyness, the feel good factor, is that the answer?

Is it worthwhile? If it feels good, is it useful, is it profitable, is it efficient, is it productive. Or does it feel good? Is that enough?

A fulfilling end to a busy day, is that enough?

Tuesday 12 September 2017 Another dull, damp day in Grey Galloway. There is a window of sunlight between 10 and 1 according to the BBC weather app. I will take the bike up the hill to Auchenleck then. Now that the Grand Tour cycling season is finished I'm at a loose end. Giro Italia in May; Tour de France in July; LaVuelta in Spain in July; What a season it was. Chris Froome achieved the amazing victory of the Yellow Jersey in Le Tour and the Red Jersey in LaVuelta. A GC (General Classification) victory for SKY. Bertie Contador 3rd on his retiring Tour. Nibali, leShark, Italy 2nd for Bahrain Merida.

After 6 months to mull it over, I have stopped looking for vacancies as a Site Manager in Construction. I am now looking for a local, part time, office job, as a manager. I changed my details on search engines in accordance with this. This morning the usual 6 emails were not there. What are my reasons? My job is dirty, dangerous, and noisy. It requires working long hours. Travelling and living away from home. All of this has taken its toll on my health. I don't enjoy it anymore.

Thursday 14 September 2017 Following a bit more research into Mum's family history this morning. Mum named Marjory (with a y) Dickson was born on 2 December 1931 in hospital at Balornock Road, Glasgow. Her mother Jane Maxwell Manderson Dickson was residing at Barr's Cottage Cardross, Springburn District, County of Lanark. On the 8 June 1932 Jane married James Alexander Leslie, a Gamekeeper. She was living at 23 High Street, Alyth working as a Domestic Servant. On 18 February 1939 Jane married Thomas Cant Kennedy, Age 37 Estate Gardener. They both resided at 39 West End Park Street, Glasgow. Jane died aged 79 in 1989 in Lanarkshire. I don't know when and where James and Thomas died. I do know Thomas travelled by ship from New York in 1932, 7 years before they married.

Marjory (by now spelling her name Marjorie) was married on 12 November 1955 to Dad, a dental receptionist from Templedean, Haddington. The John Kennedy, Police Officer (her Mum's 2nd husband) on the Marriage Certificate was not correct. This was Thomas. Reason for my search is that I am looking for Mum's siblings. So far I have drawn a blank.

Friday 15 September 2017 This morning I was reading BBC Home page and I noticed an article saying that the new Galloway Hospital in Dumfries had a key handover ceremony the day before. The man in the photo handing over the keys on behalf of Laing O'Rourke, the main contractor was one Roger Frost, Contract Director. As I turn around in my chair I am looking at a photo of my classmates in 1980's. Stood 3 to my right with his thumb up is the very same Roger Frost. 5 years ago I came here with the idea I would work on that job. I have been there. I have done induction. The jobs never worked out. I am now thinking, if I had known Roger was the top man there things might have been different, water under the bridge now. I researched who was who on that job when it started. His name didn't come to my attention. I heard personnel changed as the job progressed. I will forgive myself by saying he got involved during the job. Done!

Monday 18 September 2017. Yesterday I did the Big Country Route on the bike for the last time of the year. Home>Auchenleck>Old Edinburgh Road>Black Loch>Loch Dee>Loch Trool>Glen Trool Coffee Shop>Wood of Cree>King George V Bridge>Home; 35 Miles up and down hill on forest roads. 5 hours. The section between Black Loch and Loch Dee is the toughest. After 3 hours your strength has gone. However this stretch was rewarding. I watched 3 eagles with binoculars, hovering over the crags, looking for dinner. Over all, not bad for a man who is 61 at the end of the month.

Tuesday 26 September 2017. Last weekend was very wet. I have tickets for my first visit to Wigtown Book Festival. Wigtown is a bit of an oddity. Historically it is an older town than Newton. In the early 17th century Newton is not on the map. I was told Wigtown was dying. Houses were not selling. Prices were dropping. And then the White Settlers came. People from the south, looking for a better life. The quaint, old fashioned style was appealing. The prices were appealing. The settlers bought homes to work from. Coffee Shops, Galleries, Book shops. The Book Festival grew. I diverse.

Saturday I went to see a talk by Declan Murphy, the jockey and ghost writer Ami Rao about the book Centaur. His life, the terrible accident he had at Haydock in 1974, and his recovery. I was a bit early so I had a look around town in the wet. I had a quick drink in the Galloway Arms. The talk was in the Festival marquee. It was filling up and by the time our hosts entered there was 160 seated. Pauleen McLean, BBC Arts correspondent interviewed Declan Murphy and Ami Rao. I couldn't help but notice that Ami was very attractive and exotic. Brendan started by saying he had turned away 2 offers to write his story. I immediately understood why he didn't turn away Ami. I felt I knew Brendan because I have worked with so many young Irishmen recently. I am a horse racing fan. He still had the single minded determination of an elite racer. The talk was enjoyable and I will now read the book in full. The following day it rained all day again. I went to "The Art of Failing. Notes from the Underdog" by Anthony McGowan. This was different to yesterday. Anthony turned out to be a shambolic, self-deprecating character. He had a good sense of humour and many funny stories. Most were at his own expense. He had post it notes to mark passages he wanted to read. Immediately one fell to the floor and he lost his place. It was funny watching the audience reaction. The locals sat straight backed, tight lipped, with no declaration of approval. This must have been quite intimidating for the poor lad from West Hampstead. The settlers are more inclusive. That's a good thing for Wigtown. It needs this injection of enthusiasm. So does Penninghame.

Saturday 30 September 2017 was my 61st birthday. It was shaping up to be a quiet one. Radio 1 was celebrating its 50th birthday. Tony Blackburn was still around to celebrate. I got the papers; watched the last Malaysian Grand Prix. Max Verstappen won for Red Bull. Louis Hamilton is still winning championship for Mercedes. Sebastien Vettel is starting to lose the plot for Ferrari. It only seems a few years since the track was established. The Malaysian government has decided it's not economically viable to stage the Grand Prix in future. A Grand Folly by Bernie Ecclestone before he left F1. I have decided not to be an F1 fan in future after the Paradise Papers revealed Louis Hamilton's tax avoidance scam when he bought a private jet. It's a pity. I have been a fan since the 60s. Recently it has lost its appeal. There is some classy horse racing at Newmarket and Chantilly this weekend. Enable, ridden by Frankie Dettori, John Gosden, Francesca Cumani. Thankfully Irish Raiders did not take too many spoils. However the Saudis did. Sport of Kings it is. I took a phone call from Leyla at 4pm. She said look out the window. There was Leyla and Bekka sat outside in her little red Peugeot. They had driven 4 hours from Kirkcaldy to say hello on my birthday. What a lovely surprise. They were looking fabulously turned out. I had a quick tidy up and we walked down to the pub. The girls always turn a few heads when they visit. Pete, David and Davey were in the Gallow. I would not have made anything of my birthday had the girls not been there. We had drinks and dined then headed home to watch X Factor. Big night in Penninghame!

Monday 2 October 2017. I said I would go back to work now. I have no desire to go back to the building trade. I have looked regularly at the Job Boards for the last 6 months. Nothing has appealed. I have not had a response to anything I applied for. I can honestly say I have never had a good job in Scotland. I am staying here now whatever. I recently saw that CV library that I use are looking for a home based sales admin for Scotland. This got me thinking that agencies are around Dumfries & Galloway but not in the county. The county is vast. It got me thinking. Why don't I establish a job agency particularly for Dumfries & Galloway. I did some research and found the agencies that operate are from outside and not good quality. Local knowledge is a valuable thing in a large and diverse region. Yes work is thin on the ground. A one man agency does not require a great deal of work. I am now speaking to web designers who have produced web sites for recruitment agencies. I have looked into grants that are available. My savings is dwindling. As usual there is a lot of talk about grants. When you look into it that's all it is. Going forward I will have to stretch my savings like an elastic band. After some research I decided not to pursue this option. I decided the cost of maintaining an up to date web site would outweigh the benefits.

Saturday 7 October 2017. I have been down to the paper shop to get the new weekend "I". It claims to have TV listings for the week. Of course it does not. I will revert back to the Guardian which does. Today I will be watching with interest. The Lombardia cycling and Horse Racing from Ascot and Newmarket. I won't go to the pub this weekend. I watched Bobby Davro "In Therapy" on Channel 5 last night. I am not a fan but I was impressed with his performance. It made me think. He is my generation. He is an impressionist and TV personality, very successful in his day, down on his luck now, divorced, girlfriend problems. Work is not coming in, lonely, drinking more than he should. Therapist Mandy Saligari advised Bobby that he was by nature a "people pleaser." She bluntly said to him. Have you had a drink today? He admitted he had. She said she could smell it. She admitted to him she had treatment for alcohol addiction. She asked him about his drinking over several sessions. Bobby steadfastly refused to accept her opinion that he was an alcoholic. He said he enjoyed a drink. Not to excess. It did not affect his life. He drank every day. The whole thing made me think. When does someone who says they enjoy a drink become an alcoholic? Most households that I know have a stock of alcohol that is regularly used. I enjoy a daily drink. I regularly go without to test that I can. Am I an alcoholic? I don't think so. She wanted Bobby to attend AA meetings. He disagreed and did not go. The whole thing made me think. Where's the line? When do you cross it? In my experience it has changed from the generation I started drinking in, to now. Is it a gender thing? I went to therapy with

Daisy to try to avoid divorce. I felt the female therapist empathised with Daisy and criticised me. I think that was wrong and did not help. Again, is this something that changes from one generation to the next? Is it a gender thing? I think I am a "people pleaser" when I am with people. After a while I start to think. Hang on. What about me? It took me till I was in my 50's to realise this. I will be charming and attentive to loved ones for 3 years typically. Once I realise it is not reciprocated. I analyse them more, and log the pros and cons of the relationship. At the 5 year mark if all is not well, it's over, and I go back to being single, and selfish. My father was a people pleaser who let people walk all over him. Everyone loved him. I vowed from a young age not be like him. My mother died unhappy. Did I make things better? Probably not. I now drink alcohol three days per week.

Wednesday 11 October 2017 I am a bit concerned that my Journal entries become influenced by the book I am reading, "The Art of Failing" by Alistair McGowan. I went to see his talk at Wigtown Book Festival. I follow him on Twitter now. I did not get my book signed as writers probably think everyone queuing up for a signing are potentially a stalker. His book is showing me that writers at the bottom of the food chain have similar eccentric, shambolic ways, funny but often tragic. Not admirable. I have been struggling with what to do with my journal. Is it just something to occupy myself in later years? Some do crosswords or puzzles. Others take up serious addictions to speed their end in a dramatic flourish. Anyway I have been reluctant to make the work public so long as it is fact. I need to convert it to fiction. So the UK is going to become North America. To inject some international glamour into the proceedings Minnigaff is Malibu, Dundee is Chicago, Edinburgh is Boston, Bristol is San Francisco, and London is New York. The McCs are the McClains. Other fictitious families will be Maxwells, Leslies, Frasers, Dicksons. I hope the change does not become too unlikely to manage. Here goes.

Silly Wi Poems

London

I was watching Live At The Apollo on TV

Looking at the audience made me think

Different generation out and about in London now

I am not part of it

Different sense of humour

Different everything

Young bright eyed politically correct non judgmental

Would they feel robbed if I shared their amusement?

How long does the IT crowd last

More than a washing machine?

Less than a fridge?

More than an Iphone for sure

But not as long as Tony Blackburn

On 30 September2017 Tony Blackburn celebrates 50 years broadcasting on national Radio established on 30 September 1967 at 7am when Tony opened the breakfast show on Radio1.

The Killing Fields (V)

Man breeds, nourishes the beasts that roam

His daily tormentors

He is a slave to their needs

And they will make him suffer

Every day of their short lives

They will not go easy

Grudgingly they accommodate

And sometimes flee

For they will die young

So sweet when young

And tender on the plate

A life with no name

Bloodstock

When them that are high bred

Fall in love & marry

Those of humble birth

Family are perplexed

American Dream 1955-2020 AJ McClain

Airs and graces forgotten

Tradition set aside

Rules and conventions ignored

The dice is spun

Where it lands cannot be predicted

Only time will tell

Nature will prevail

Children will arrive

The fruits of their love

For better or worse

For richer or poorer

The tree will grow for as long as blood is warm

Judgement will come in time

As sure as the horse that runs truer and faster

And has no vices

Is said to be a good horse and goes down in history

The bad horse is forgotten

What do you do?

That's a very good question

I was a student

I studied numbers

Not by choice, by accident

I chose to work with my hands

Creating furniture & buildings

And then I managed men

Men & Buildings

And now I am a wordsmith

A poet, a writer, storyteller, lyricist

I walk, explore, cycle, and think

I talk little

But to all intents and purposes

I am nothing, I am no one

Laundry Bay

Lazing in the sun at Brad's

Listening to the wind in the grass

And the chimes of the yacht rigging

A sand yacht races by

Kite swirling in the wind

Buckets and spades

Rock pooling

Nets no longer used

Too few salmon to net

Poles like forgotten teeth in the sand

On the horizon the shimmering incoming tide

Timeless blue sky brushed with feather and mackerel clouds

Into The Wild

(A film directed by Sean Penn about Christopher McCandless)

In the past men, women and children

Went out in the wilderness

Looking for a life that is free

From rules and oppression

Some lived and prospered

Some died looking

Better that

Than not to have tried

And lived in torment

In a life less satisfied

Newton's Little Problem

Rain, rain, rain in August

Soaking in the land

And soaking in, again

Flooding out and down

Deeper, faster, more

Nothing slowing it down

Quicker into town

And out to sea

I'm glad they took the bridge down

Else, where would we be

Shymie

11 August 2017

Shymie will not be forgotten

She dominates the first four pages of Google

And that's without telling her story

Her story is a screenplay for a movie

Shymie is not defined in the dictionary

But we all have our definition

Shymie is the dance of Tahitian girls

Shymie was the force that was a gang of young men

in a town I grew up in Dundee

Shymie is the woman Ian met in the Nova

The Mother of Acarman Road

The Proud Mother of Beth Amy Claire

Shymie was the embodiment of the 60's

She was there in the prime of her life

And experienced it to the full

Shymie brought us all together to have fun

American Dream 1955-2020 AJ McClain

She had 50 things to do before you die 25 years ago

I bet she still had 50 things to do when she left us

When I think of Shymie

I remember happy days on the Sussex Downs

At Goodwood Festival

And of course Shymies extended family

At Acarman Road

Goodbye and God bless Shymie

You are always in our hearts

Cycling into Kintra

The landscape is vast

Weather in turmoil

Waves crashing on the beach

Beasts stare

A huge flock of geese take to the sky as I approach

A crescendo of noise

Downwardly Mobile

I'm a middle class boy

Who lives in a house

In a poor part of town

That fits my needs

It's warm and it has no vices

People say

But your only renting

And I know what they mean

But I don't have to explain

It's all that I want

And it suits my needs

It's warm and it has no vices

Garden Birds

I like to feed the birds

Finches, sparrows, tits are welcome

Pigeons, doves and even pheasants

But Jackdaws

I'd like to get a gun and shoot them

And hang their corpses up to dry

And send a message to the rest.

Different Day

A dog barked early

The child woke up crying

The parents got up

The birds got up

The neighbourhood got up

Everyone was annoyed

Routine was upset

Where did it end?

Another Different Day

Summer rain makes the blocked gutter drip

It wakes the child who cries

The cat wakes

The parents wake

The neighbourhood got up

Everyone was annoyed

Routine was upset

Where did it end?

Bad Weather in Newton

If you wake up and the rains blowing from the East

Stay inside and quell your ambition

Don't be impatient

Stay inside and wait for it to pass

For it will in time

Do these jobs inside that you ken aboot

Then go to bed

It's as simple as that in Newton.

Fallen Stock

If your out on your bike

And a truck comes round the corner

And you read "Fallen Stock"

Don't despair

Give the driver a wave

Take a breath as he goes by

What's that smell?

The smell of death

Not the death of your investments

In faraway places

Or profitable funds in successful business

Your pensions safe

It's some poor beast that's fallen dead

He'll scoop it up

And bid it a fond farewell

And recycle the remains

For future prosperity.

Tracks of my Years

ABBA Chiquitita The Winner Takes It All

Al Green How Can You Mend a Broken Heart

Average White Band Lets Go Round Again

Bob Dylan Lay Lady Lay

Beatles Blackbird

Calvin Harris Feels Summer

David Bowie Heroes

Diana Ross Reflections

Dionne Warwick Heartbreaker

Divine Comedy Something for the Weekend

Eagles Desperado

Elvis Presley Suspicious Minds

Elvis Costello I Don't Want to go to (Chelsea)

ELO Mr Blue Sky

Eric Clapton Layla Wonderful Tonight

Fleetwood Mac Rumours

Glen Campbell Wichita Lineman Phoenix

Hermans Hermits I'm Into Something Good

Hollies The Air That I Breath

Housemartins Happy Hour

Ian Dury Reasons To Be Cheerful Part 3

John Lennon Jealous Guy

KC & the Sunshine Band Get Down Tonight

Kool & The Gang Fresh

Kim Wilde Water on Glass

Led Zeppelin Stairway to Heaven

Massive Attack Unfinished Symphony

Miles Davies Blue in Green

Neil Young Only Love Can Break Your Heart

Radiohead Paranoid Android

Rolling Stones Little T&A

Santana Samba Pa Ti

Van Morrison Sweet Thing

Verve Bitter Sweet Symphony

Whitney Houston I Have Nothing

ZZ Top Got Me Under Pressure

Last Will and Testament of A J McClain 5 October 2017

Anything I have after my death is to be divided equally between my three children Leyla, Bekka and Jim. I am to be cremated. A service to be at Monnigaff Church. My ashes to be scattered at GeorgeV Bridge. Music, All Things Bright and Beautiful, Desperado, Stairway to Heaven,

10321890R00087

Printed in Germany
by Amazon Distribution
GmbH, Leipzig